DEMON

Davy, gazing throu[...] [...]g materialize in the gloom, a vague, grotesque shape that loomed larger by the moment, acquiring the silhouette of a horse and rider, but a horse and rider unlike any Davy had ever beheld. For both man and beast were immense, the horse an enormous black stallion whose nostrils and eyes were flared wide, the man a hulking brute from whose broad shoulders flapped a long, coarse cloak.

All of this Davy noted in an instant. They were charging straight at the window but he expected them to stop short. No sane rider would do otherwise. Grasping his rifle, he tried to shout a warning, a shout that died in his throat, smothered by shock.

Demonic laughter rang out. Everyone swivelled toward the source. And the next second the horse smashed into the window at full gallop, shattering the glass into thousands of tiny shards.

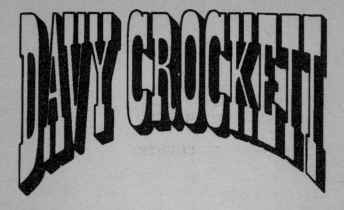

TEXICAN TERROR

←――――――――――――――――――――→

David Thompson

LEISURE BOOKS NEW YORK CITY

To Judy, Joshua, and Shane

A LEISURE BOOK®

May 1998

Published by

Dorchester Publishing Co., Inc.
276 Fifth Avenue
New York, NY 10001

ISBN 0-8439-4389-0

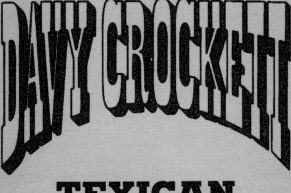

TEXICAN
TERROR

Chapter One

One moment the prairie was peaceful, quiet. The next, up out of a gully rushed six grungy horsemen. Riders in grimy buckskins and greasy homespun garb. Men who were armed to the teeth. Men who bore the cruel stamp of vicious and cunning natures on their swarthy faces.

Davy Crockett was taken completely by surprise. Lost in thought, he had been drifting southward, on the lookout for San Antonio de Bexar. Something about that name appealed to him. It had a nice ring to the ear. Once he reached it, he could give serious thought to returning to his beloved Tennessee and his wife and family. A step long overdue.

The brawny Irishman was thinking about Elizabeth and their kids when the riders streamed out of the gully. Startled, he nonetheless leveled his rifle and placed his thumb on the hammer. Liz, he called her, in honor of his wife.

The six men acted indifferent to the threat. Fanning out into a crescent, they closed in, halting about twenty feet out. In the center was a husky man whose bristly beard and dark, beady eyes lent him the aspect of a bear. A mean bear, if the gleam in those eyes was any indication. "Howdy, hoss," he declared gruffly. "Fancy comin' on another white man out here in the middle of nowhere."

"Yes, fancy that," tittered a scarecrow who was missing three of his upper front teeth. He also had a nervous tic; his left eyelid kept twitching. "Nice horse you've got there, stranger. Nice rifle and pistols, too."

Davy Crockett was no fool. Smiles and banter did not deceive him. Although a newcomer to the vast, sprawling Spanish-ruled land of Texas, he had heard about human wolves like these. Freebooters, they were called. Which was just another word to describe robbers and killers. Vermin who strayed over the border onto Spanish soil to prey on anyone and everyone. Of late the raids had become so widespread and brutal that the people of Nacogdoches were reportedly thinking of abandoning their East Texas town, one of only three established communities in all of Texas.

The husky freebooter's beady eyes darted beyond Crockett and swept the plain. "You all alone, hoss?"

"I wish I may be shot if I'm not," Davy lied. He was not about to tell them about the others, in his party. "On my way to San Antonio. You gents wouldn't happen to know how far that would be?"

"Oh, a day's ride or so," answered the leader. "You should strike on some farms sooner than that."

"Yes." The scarecrow snickered. "Plenty of sod tillers movin' on in of late. Most don't even have permission."

"Are you boys farmers too?" Davy asked, playing the innocent. He pretended to overlook the sly glances they exchanged at his expense.

"Not exactly," the leader said smugly. His bushy brows knit. "That's quite a drawl you've got there, mister. You wouldn't happen to be from Kentucky, by any chance?"

"No. I'm from the great sovereign state of Tennessee," Davy boasted. "Land of milk and honey. And the prettiest womenfolk you're likely to see this side of a Turkoman's harem."

The leader casually rested both hands on the rifle slanted across his thighs. "Got yourself a way with words, pilgrim."

"Speechifying comes natural to the Irish," Davy quipped. "When we're in our cups, we'll talk your ears off." He was stalling, hoping against hope his friends would realize what had happened and come to his aid. If not, he was as good as dead. Six to one were impossible odds.

The scarecrow was fidgeting as if he had ants in his britches. "Enough jabberin', Spike. Let's get on with it, shall we? I want to be back across the border by the end of the week, you know."

The husky leader frowned. "Damn you, Horace. You're always so impatient. One day it'll be the death of you." To Davy he said, "It's like this, friend. We aim to take your horse and your guns and all your effects. So make it easy and fork 'em over. 'Cause if you don't, you'll be worm food before you can bat an eye."

As if on cue, most of the freebooters trained rifles on the Tennessean. Horace cocked his and sighted squarely on Crockett's forehead. "I love to see brains gush out," he mentioned matter-of-factly.

Davy had frozen. To paraphrase the Bible, there was a time for a man to fight and a time for him to try to talk his way out of one. This particular instance fell into the latter category. "Now, hold on, fellers," he said good-naturedly. "You'd steal from a fellow white man? You'd leave him at the mercy of wild beasts and Indians?"

"Sure would," Horace said.

Spike sighed loudly. "Sorry, friend. It's what we do.

Pickin's is easy on this side of the Sabine River. Ain't no law to speak of. And there aren't enough Spanish soldiers to patrol everywhere at once.''

Horace was so eager to squeeze the trigger, he trembled in anticipation. ''Tell him your life's story, why don't you? What's gotten into you, Spike? He's just another no-account would-be settler who should have stayed to home.''

''Refresh my memory, Horace,'' Spike said testily. ''Which one of us is top dog here?''

The scarecrow's head snapped up. Genuine fear replaced his cocky attitude. ''Hold on, now. Don't go gettin' riled. I didn't mean nothin'. Honest. If you want to pass the time of day with this jasper, be my guest.''

''That's better,'' Spike said.

Davy cleared his throat. ''If all you want is my possibles and my animal, go right ahead and take them. I won't lift a finger to stop you.''

Horace tittered again. ''Wouldn't help you none if you did, southerner. It didn't help that dirt farmer we raided last night, either.''

Spike moved so quickly, his body was a blur. The stock of his rifle swept up and around and caught Horace on the shoulder, dumping the skinny freebooter from the saddle.

Squawking like a stricken hen, Horace tumbled. Almost immediately he bounded to his feet, but he was shaken and it showed. ''Now, what in tarnation did you do that for?''

''Be thankful it's all I did,'' Spike said. ''You should have the devil to pay for jawin' too damn much.'' He leaned toward the scarecrow and growled, ''One of these days I'm liable to sew that mouth of yours shut with catgut.''

The squabble worked in Davy's favor. Every second the freebooters squandered increased the likelihood of his traveling companions noticing. He had to be ready. To that end, he slid his feet from the stirrups without being obvious. ''Seems to me you boys have picked a rough life for yourselves,'' he prattled. ''From what I hear, neither government cottons much to your kind. Sooner or later they're bound to get you.''

''Later rather than sooner,'' Spike predicted. ''I know all the tricks. Got my start back with Nolan, rustling horses.'' The Irishman's blank expression prompted him to explain, ''Phil Nolan. Don't tell me you never heard of him? Hell, he was the living terror of Texas for a good number of years. Ran the Spaniards ragged, he did. Until one day the soldiers ambushed him and sent his ears to the governor.''

Davy could not help musing that it was a fitting fate for a living terror, but he held his tongue. Shifting his weight, he tensed.

Horace muttered up a storm. Averting his gaze from Spike, he stepped to his sorrel to climb back on. ''Fine state of affairs,'' he groused aloud, ''when your own pard hauls off and hits you.''

Spike nodded at Crockett. ''All right, friend. Hand over your belongings. And no tricks, you hear? Not if you want to go on breathin'.''

The freebooters were fooling no one. Davy knew they could not let him live. One of the reasons the renegades had lasted so long was their ironclad rule to never, ever leave witnesses. He started to extend Liz, even though he had no intention of letting them take her. ''Here you go.''

At that juncture one of the other cutthroats stiffened and peered intently northward. ''Say? What's that flash yonder?''

The crack of a rifle punctuated the question. Davy heard the distinct thud of the heavy ball smashing into the freebooter's skull. It burst out the other side, showering hair and gore in a wide circle. For a few heartbeats the lifeless husk sat rigid, then the man oozed from his horse like melted butter.

It was Davy's cue. Leaping from his mount, he fired in midair, Liz booming and spewing smoke and hot lead. Total shock etched Spike's bristly features as the shot smashed into his sternum. Davy did not see the cutthroat fall, for the next instant the ground rushed up to meet him, and Davy rolled. Letting go of the rifle, he grabbed a pistol, aware that bedlam had erupted above.

Men cursed lustily and snapped off return fire. One screamed in agony. Horses whinnied and shied. To the north other rifles opened up, and for a bit the *smack-smack-smack* of bullets was constant.

In the brief time it took for Davy to surge into a crouch, half the freebooters had been blasted into eternity. Horace was still unscathed, though, and reining his mount around to flee. Davy took aim. The scarecrow spotted him and clawed at a flintlock.

Davy fired before the barrel could clear. His .55-caliber smoothbore packed a powerful wallop, and at that range the shot lifted Horace clean off the saddle and flung him to the grass in a wretched, crumpled heap.

Only one freebooter escaped. He did so by slipping over the side of his mount, Comanche-style, and racing to the east at breakneck speed.

The Irishman did not give chase. For one thing, his horse was weary from days of constant travel. For another, he did not care to be separated from his friends, not when they were so close to their destination.

Unlimbering the other flintlock, Davy moved to a man who wheezed and writhed in torment. A spurting hole high on the chest testified to a severe lung wound. "You're not long for this world, mister. Want me to put you out of your misery?"

The man stopped writhing long enough to vigorously shake his head.

"Suit yourself," Davy said. "But you're only going to suffer a lot longer." Relieving the doomed soul of weapons, Davy set them aside. As he straightened, a commotion heralded the arrival of the unlikely bunch fate had thrown him in with.

First and foremost was Flavius Harris. As the Irishman's best friend, Flavius had been at Crockett's side every long, harrowing step of the way from far distant Tennessee—and regretted every minute of it. When Davy first proposed going on a "little gallivant," Flavius had imagined being gone two weeks at the most. Yet it had been over two months since Flavius last set eyes on his quaint cabin and domineering wife, Matilda. Not to mention his prized coon dogs.

"Consarn it, you gave me a scare," Flavius said as he pounded up. "What were you thinking? Why didn't you just hightail it back to us the moment those scum appeared?"

Nothing scared Flavius more than the thought of losing Davy. The notion of finding his way back to Tennessee alone was downright terrifying. Flavius was no fool. He knew his limitations. Without Crockett, they would not have survived as long as they had.

"Are you all right, Davy?" asked a stunning blonde who rode a bay bareback. Heather Dugan had been stranded on the prairie with her daughter, and if not for the two Tennesseans she would not be alive.

"I thought those varmints had you for sure," commented the pretty bundle riding double with Heather. A product of city life, young Becky had taken to talking like the frontiersmen. "Good thing Mr. Tanner is a fine shot."

Farley Tanner was a Texican, one of the rare new breed of hardy settlers carving homesteads out of the wilderness. The Spanish government had granted him an extensive land grant, which he planned to one day develop into a sprawling ranch. A broad-shouldered, strapping man, he favored a pair of elaborate ivory-handled flintlocks that were wedged under a wide studded belt. He was also a fine shot with a rifle.

On the same horse, clinging to her brother's arms, sat Marcella Tanner. Just over a week before she had been a captive of the dreaded Comanches. Thanks to her brother and a small group from San Antonio, aided by Davy and Flavius, she was free and safe. And as happy as a lark.

The other two members of their party were Ormbach, a farmer, and Taylor, whose gray-streaked hair marked him as someone of experience and wisdom. Once a hunter by trade, he had plans to build a successful business in San Antonio.

Davy regarded them all fondly. Together they had fought Comanches, battled the elements, resisted blistering heat and parching thirst. Mutual hardship had forged a bond neither time nor distance would ever sever. In the back of his mind Davy was toying with the idea of convincing Liz to pack up their brood and move to Texas. An unlikely proposition, what with all her kin being in Tennessee.

Taylor and Ormbach also rode double, the result of having only five mounts for the eight of them. Now Taylor slid down and cracked a grin. "At least we have all the horses we need, with some to spare."

"And we're only a day out of San Antonio," Davy said, repeating the information Spike had imparted.

"That's my guess," Taylor agreed. Nudging one of the dead freebooters with a toe, he remarked, "We've done Texas a favor today. Dirty business, but there's no telling how many poor unfortunates these polecats murdered."

"There are more of them?" Flavius asked. He recalled one of the Texicans saying something to that effect, and he anxiously scanned the tall grass.

"A lot more," Farley Tanner said. "No one knows exactly how many. Moses Austin told me he reckons upwards of two hundred. This was a small bunch."

Ormbach snorted. "Small bands, big bands, they're all the same. Vultures, scavenging off the sweat and toil of decent folks. Wouldn't upset me none if every last one was skinned alive and staked out on anthills, Injun-style.''

The farmer's sentiments confirmed for Davy how intensely the Texicans felt about the marauders. Some fifteen years before in 1805, the state of affairs had become so wretched, with so much bloodletting and widespread mayhem, the United States and Mexican governments had sat down and ironed out an agreement to solve the crisis. Or so they thought.

Their solution was to set up a so-called neutral zone. The broad area lay between a tributary of the Red River and the Sabine. No citizens from either country were allowed into it, the idea being that this would serve as a buffer zone and stem the crimson tide.

On paper, at any rate, it was a great idea. But, as with most government brainstorms, it fell apart from its own weight. Spanish authorities did not have enough soldiers to police the zone, and American authorities couldn't be bothered.

So the freebooters had gone on butchering and plundering to their hearts' content. And now they were poised to take over a full third of Texas unless something was done. Or so the rumor mill had it.

Davy escorted the women a short distance farther along while the Texican men stripped the bodies. No burials were held. No religious words were said over the corpses. The freebooters were left where they had sprawled. Presently scavengers would catch the scent. Coyotes and buzzards and other creatures would converge. In a few days not so much as a single shred of flesh would remain.

Becky tried to look back, but her mother gripped her shoulders.

''Don't you dare, child! I won't have you staring at naked men.'' Heather swung her daughter around. ''It's bad enough, all the killing and ugliness you've seen. I have to draw the line somewhere.''

Marcy Tanner was not upset at all. Glancing over a slender shoulder, she yawned, then brushed at her golden bangs. "If you've seen one naked man, you've seen them all," she said more coldly than Flavius would have thought her capable of. "But you're wise to spare the girl from the worst of frontier life for as long as you can, Heather. It can be positively awful at times. Certainly not fit for a lady like yourself."

"I'm hardly a lady," Heather said, and did not elaborate.

Flavius did not bother to look back either. Truth to tell, the sight of blood made him downright squeamish. Oh, he'd fought in the Creek War and been involved in more than his share of savage scrapes since. But he could never get used to it, as Davy and so many acquaintances seemed to.

The extra mounts were an unexpected godsend, one Flavius would have been much more grateful for weeks before. The more horses they had, the sooner they'd reach San Antonio. And the sooner they reached San Antonio, the quicker they would be on their way to Tennessee. Flavius could hardly wait.

Presently the Texicans returned. Two of the horses were pressed into service as beasts of burden, laden with blankets and clothes and the like. Among the booty was a parfleche crammed with pemmican. Where the freebooters had obtained it was a mystery.

"See these beads?" Ormbach said. "It's Cheyenne, or I'm the Queen of England."

"You're loco, is what you are," Taylor countered. "It's Kiowa, plain and simple. I should know. I lived with them a short while during my buffalo-hunting days."

Davy did not have an opinion on the matter. The tribes west of the Mississippi were all new to him. All he could say about them for sure was the important lesson he'd learned during his brief captivity among the Sioux—namely, that the Indians weren't the unbridled brutes many in the States painted them as. In fact, red men were a lot like whites, sharing many of the same dreams and fears. For the rest of his born days he would never forget the young couple who befriended him at the risk of incurring the wrath of their brethren.

But then, Davy never had been an inveterate Indian hater. He wasn't one of those who believed the only good Indian was a dead one. Even after he joined the campaign against the Creeks, he never despised them as a race. He had simply been doing his part to ensure no more massacres like the one at Fort Mimms ever took place again.

Soon the tired travelers were all mounted, forging southward once more. Based on the position of the sun, Davy reckoned the time to be between one and two.

Earlier, about noon, they had halted to briefly rest in a shallow basin sixty yards north of the spot where the freebooters had jumped him. It was a sheer stroke of luck he had headed out slightly ahead of the others, or the cutthroats might have shot all of them dead before they knew what hit them.

Hooves hammered as Taylor rode up alongside Davy's bay. "So how soon do you aim to light a shuck for home, Crockett?" he inquired good-naturedly.

Davy liked the older Texican. Hell, he liked all of them. They were rugged, independent cusses, much like himself in nature and temperament. Texas was the new frontier, and to it flocked frontiersmen from all across the country. How could he not feel the same allure they did?

No doubt about it. Texas was intoxicating. In size it was beyond belief, a country unto itself. But its real charm lay in its exotic beauty, natural splendor few states could rival. Davy had crossed countless miles of gently waving prairie grass, grass growing lush from rich brown soil. He had crossed countless clear streams gurgling along sandy bottoms. He had seen giant pecan trees, and many others he had no name for yet were magnificent in their own right.

Yes, sir. Texas was special. Men like Farley Tanner knew it. So did Moses Austin, whom Davy was anxious to meet. Word had it that Austin was going to set himself up as an *empresario* and arrange for an influx of new settlers from America.

Davy had not mentioned this to Flavius, of course. His friend was already put out with him for the unusual turns their gallivant had taken. No, Davy aimed to consult with Austin on the sly.

Now, answering Taylor, Davy said, "We won't be leaving for four or five days, maybe more. We're plumb tuckered out after the ordeal we've been through."

Flavius Harris overheard and promptly spurred his horse forward. "Four or five days?" he bleated. "Why wait that long? I can be ready to leave the morning after we reach San Antonio."

Taylor smiled. "And miss out on our famous Texican hospitality? I've got a Mexican friend who loves to throw fiestas. All he needs is an excuse. You'll eat and drink until you bust a gut. Plus meet some of the prettiest *senoritas* in all of Mexico."

Flavius didn't give a hoot about the women. Chasing skirts wasn't for him. But the thought of all that food and drink made his senses swim. How long had it been since he last ate a real meal? he asked himself, and was jolted to realize it had been so long, he couldn't recollect exactly when. "What kind of food?"

"You name it. Beef so thick and juicy you can never get enough. Venison sometimes. Beans, pumpkins, tomatoes, chilies. Porridge. Hot chocolate. *Tortillas, enchiladas, puchero,* and more."

Flavius did not know what those last three were, but he'd heard enough. His stomach rumbled loudly enough to be heard in St. Louis and his mouth watered like a gushing geyser. Food was his main joy in life, his passion, his constant craving. "Well," he said, his voice oddly strained, "I wouldn't want to be accused of declining your hospitality. I suppose staying four or five days wouldn't hurt."

Davy hid a grin when Taylor winked at him. He was in the Texican's debt.

"Life here is grand," Taylor waxed enthusiastic. "There are regular *fandangos*, or dances. Or maybe your prefer horse races. Or cockfights. Believe me. There is something for everyone."

"You make Texas sound like the Garden of Eden," Davy joked.

"I swear to the Almighty, Crockett, at times I truly believe it is."

Trees appeared ahead, a sure sign of another waterway. A sparkling stream enabled them to water the horses and fill water skins taken from the freebooters. Within half an hour they were under way, eager to cover as many miles as they could before night fell.

Becky was astride the smallest of the animals, a frisky mare. She joined the Irishman to announce, "Mother told me we're going to stay here a good long spell. I think it's because she likes Mr. Tanner."

Only someone of her tender years would make so brazen a statement. "Could be," Davy allowed. Everyone was aware of the keen attraction Heather and Farley shared. They were like lovestruck birds, always brushing elbows, rubbing shoulders. Davy would be amazed if there wasn't a wedding in San Antonio before the year was out.

"I don't rightly know if I'll like this place much," Becky commented.

"Why wouldn't you?"

"They speak a different language. Their clothes aren't the

same. Even the food is different, I hear. What if I don't fit in? Or they don't like me?''

Davy was reminded of his stay with the Sioux. ''People are people, Becky. Doesn't matter what they eat or how they dress or how they talk. Peel all of that away and everyone is more or less the same.''

''Never thought of it that way.''

More and more vegetation sprouted. Clusters of trees expanded into tracts of verdant woodland. Twice they spied deer. Once, several buffalo in the distance. The sun had just blazed the western horizon vivid hues of red, orange, and yellow when Davy's keen eyes spied something else.

Bearing rapidly toward them from the southeast came a column of men. Sunshine reflected off glittering buttons and sword hilts. A banner fluttered from a lance, but it was too far off for Davy to make it out.

''Uh-oh,'' Taylor said, reining up. ''This could be trouble. The four of you don't have legal papers yet.''

''So?'' Flavius said.

''So those are Spanish soldiers. And if the officer in charge is the coyote I suspect, he'd as soon throw illegal Americans in prison as look at them.''

Chapter Two

The lancers were a magnificent sight, Davy Crockett had to admit. Although both the mounts and the men were caked with dust, it did not detract from their appearance or their bearing. Sitting their saddles ramrod straight, heads high, lances upraised, they filed with precision across the prairie.

In the lead was a rake-lean Spaniard whose hawkish features and hooked nose hinted at an aggressive nature. Flashing eyes surveyed the world with grim suspicion. He had a pencil-thin mustache waxed to a sheen, and a neatly cropped beard that jutted from an angular chin.

"It's just like I feared," Taylor said out of the corner of his mouth. "Capitán Jose Barragan. A regular son of a bitch if ever there was one." To the other Texicans he said urgently, "Quick. Before they get here. Move up in front."

Ormbach, Farley, and Marcy immediately did so, forming a row with Taylor on the left end. They waited calmly, but Flavius noticed that both Taylor and Farley fingered their rifles, and Farley loosened one of those expensive pistols of his.

Captain Barragan did not give the command to halt until the lancers were almost on top of the Texicans. He regarded the four with open disdain, then slowly removed his gauntlets and swatted them against his leg, raising puffs of dust. Taking his sweet time, he at last coughed, then said suavely, "Greetings, Senor Tanner, Senor Taylor. I am glad your bid to save the lovely Marcella was successful."

Farley Tanner's jaw muscles twitched. "No thanks to you, Captain. I asked you for help but you refused, if you'll recall."

Barragan sniffed. "I am a soldier, Senor Tanner. I must follow orders. And my orders are to avoid provoking the Comanches at all costs. There are many more of them than there are of us. If the tribe should ever take it into their heads to drive us out, we would be helpless to resist."

Taylor spoke up. "So you do nothing? Even when they raid our settlements and carry off our women? What about Spain's promise to protect the settlers? Doesn't that count for something?"

The Spaniard idly gestured at the forty soldiers behind him. "What would you have me do, senor? Go up against the entire Comanche nation with this pitiful handful? Be reasonable, eh? I do the best I can with the limited resources I am given."

Taylor wasn't satisfied. "What good did it do us to swear an oath of allegiance to Spain if she won't treat us the same as Spanish citizens? You know as well as I do that if it had been, say, Senorita Varga, the daughter of the *alcalde*, who was taken, the army would not rest until she was safe and sound."

"Ah. Now you touch on politics," Barragan said. "As a humble soldier, I try to avoid becoming entangled in that web." His mustache quirked upward. "As for your oath, without it you would not be permitted to remain in Texas." He mimicked Taylor's tone. "You know as well as I do Spain has been very generous to you Americans. Senor Tanner, for one, now owns more land than most native Mexicans. And all for taking a simple oath.''

Farley bristled. ''I don't like what you're implying, Capitán. Spain has no objection to American settlers moving in. Why should you?''

In a twinkling, Barragan's features rippled into a mask of spite, betraying his true feelings. ''Because Spain does not know Americans like I do, senor. The officials who decide policy are far away, in Mexico City. They do not see the hunger in the eyes of those like yourself. They do not sense as I do that your kind will not be satisfied until you have taken all of this land for yourselves.'' He paused. ''I trust you have heard of Senor Austin's grand scheme to bring in hundreds more? That is just the beginning, I fear.''

Tanner appeared ready to argue, but Taylor smoothed his ruffled feathers by saying, ''Don't take it so serious, Farley. I doubt the good capitán holds a grudge against us personal-like. He just doesn't want to see the apple cart upset, is all.''

Barragan smiled without warmth. ''What a quaint way to phrase the situation, Senor Taylor. But true. I would not like for the status quo to be changed.''

Marcy had been uncommonly quiet during the exchange. Now she interjected, ''If you ask me, Captain, you're barking up the wrong tree. It's not us Americans you should worry about. It's the Mexicans. They're the ones who are talking about revolting.''

''Ah. You deign to speak to me,'' Barragan said with oily relish. ''As for the whispered revolution, it is no more than the prattle of discontented children. The Mexicans would not dare to rise up against their rightful masters. We have ruled them for hundreds of years, and we will go on ruling them for hundreds more.''

Davy found the information quite interesting. From what he

could gather, Texas, indeed all of Mexico, was a powder keg waiting to explode. All it would take was the right spark.

Captain Barragan ogled Marcella Tanner. "I am most happy to see you are alive and well. I have thought of you often since the *fandango*."

"I'm here no thanks to you," she shot back. "And if I recall rightly, your behavior at that dance was not something a true gentleman would care to remember."

Davy had never seen a man flush as deeply scarlet as the Spaniard suddenly did. Barragan visibly had to control his temper before he responded.

"As always, your acid tongue cuts me to the quick. But enough banter." Straightening, Barragan gazed directly past the Texicans at Davy, Flavius, and Heather. "I see some new faces, do I not? Perhaps, Senor Taylor, you would do me the honor of introducing me to your friends? And, naturally, they will show me their papers so I can establish they are here in Texas lawfully."

Taylor squirmed like a fish on a hook. "I'll gladly introduce them, but there are a few things you ought to know—"

Davy did not wait for the Texican to finish. Seizing the bull by the horns, as it were, he plastered a broad grin on his face and kneed the bay toward the officer while extending his right hand. "Pleased to make your acquaintance, sir," he declared merrily. "Name's Crockett. Back at home, folks call me an Indian-fighting, bear-hunting, whiskey-loving fool, so I guess that will do for an introduction as good as any other. Might I say you're just about the finest example of a soldier I've ever seen?"

It was hard to say who was more flabbergasted, the Spaniard or the four Texicans. Barragan took Davy's hand, but warily, as if he feared Davy intended to bury a dagger between his ribs.

"Cat got your tongue, old coon?" Davy said glibly. "I take

it you don't meet many Tennesseans in this neck of the woods? We're not ones for beating around the bush. We say what we mean and mean what we say.'' He pumped his arm with gusto and almost laughed at the Spaniard's comical expression. ''So what's this about us needing papers? I'm afraid, sir, we don't have any.''

''You admit it?''

''Sure do. Why not?'' Davy said, still pumping. ''We're not out to break the law. Hellfire, the only reason we're here at all is because of those ornery Comanches. They stole this lady here, and her sprout—,'' Davy indicated Heather and Becky ''—and my pard and me had to track them down. We'd never have saved them if we hadn't run into Mr. Taylor and his friends.''

Flavius Harris inwardly smiled. He could tell the Spaniard had no idea what to make of the Irishman. Small wonder. His friend had a rare gift for gab. At taverns from one end of Tennessee to the other, Davy had entertained the patrons with tall tales that were pearls to the ear. Flavius often joked that Davy could talk rings around a tree, and it was no exaggeration.

Captain Barragan grew thoughtful. ''I must confess,'' he said at length, ''it is refreshing to meet someone with your candor, Senor Crockett. But it is my duty to take you and your friends into custody, I am afraid.''

''After the favor he did you?'' Taylor said bitterly.

''How is that, senor?''

''Freebooters.'' Taylor waved to the north. ''Six of the buzzards. Largely thanks to Mr. Crockett, five of them are bleaching in the sun.''

''Oh?'' Barragan pursed his lips. ''Then you have indeed done me a favor. It is those very men I am after. They raided two farms near San Antonio. Murdered both families, and

25

raped the women." He began to tug on a glove. "How far did you say? I must retrieve the bodies."

"Not half a day's ride," Taylor said.

"*Excelente,*" the officer said.

"Hold on. You're leaving?" Davy said. "Aren't you going to arrest us? If we're breaking the law, you should."

Barragan blinked. "Fascinating. Tell me, senor. Are there many more like you back in—where did you say—Tennessee?"

"Thousands. Why?"

"Never mind." Barragan lifted his reins. "I see no need to take you into custody, senor. But I must ask what your plans are."

Davy shrugged. "We figured on resting up in San Antonio a few days, then heading for the States. My wife will have kittens if I don't mosey home before the leaves turn."

"Have kittens?" the captain repeated, and chuckled. "You Americans and your idioms. That is a new one on me. I must remember it." He clapped Davy on the shoulder. "I like you, senor. You have my permission to go on to San Antonio. Perhaps in a day or two I will look you up. I must file a report and will need certain information."

"Anything to be helpful."

Barragan glanced sharply at Taylor and Tanner. "Did you hear him, gentlemen? If more of your countrymen shared his attitude, our two peoples would get along much better. *Adiós* for now." With a crisp arc of his gauntlet, the Spaniard led the column briskly on.

Davy waved cheerily, then shifted to find Taylor gaping at him as if he were an apparition.

"That was masterful, plumb masterful."

Chuckling, Flavius moved forward. "Tell me about it. My pard is a regular humdinger. Folks say he ought to go on the stump and maybe run for the legislature, but he'd rather hunt bears than put up with all the shenanigans that go on at the statehouse.

"A man has to have some dignity," Davy allowed.

Marcy Tanner laughed. "Imagine! Telling Barragan he should take you into custody. I thought he'd pop a vein."

Her brother motioned. "Let's light a shuck before the good *capitán* has a change of heart."

In a knot they hastened along for as long as light remained. Twilight had descended and a few stars had blossomed when Taylor veered toward a wooded belt adjacent to a stream. In a small clearing they made camp. Ormbach and Taylor tended to the horses while the women built a fire and the Tennesseans and Farley Tanner roved in search of game for the supper pot.

Small wildlife was abundant. Rabbits were everywhere. Squirrels chattered at them from the haven of high branches. Birds flitted gaily about. Davy was inclined to settle for rabbit meat for a stew, but Farley insisted on trying for a deer. In a marshy bottom rank with reeds they spooked a buck and three does. The Texican snapped his rifle up, but Davy was a shade faster. At Liz's retort, the buck dropped in midjump.

Everyone was in high spirits. The worst of their ordeal was over. Soon Farley and Marcy would be reunited with their mother. Taylor and Ormbach could resume their interrupted lives.

Becky limped about, humming happily. Heather could not take her eyes off of Farley. Flavius dragged a log from the trees and sat close to the fire to watch the dripping chunks of meat slowly roast. It took every ounce of self-control he possessed not to grab a halfway-raw piece and bite into it. When Taylor came over and squatted nearby the Tennessean roused himself to ask a question that had been on his mind since parting company with the lancers.

"Say. Why'd those soldiers even bother with the freebooters? The bodies are going to be a mite ripe by the time Barragan finds them.''

''The captain wouldn't care if they were crawling with maggots,'' Taylor replied. ''He's got his own best interests at heart.''

''How so?''

''Freebooters are hardly ever caught. The last officer who brought in some dead ones was promoted and transferred to Mexico City.'' Taylor poked a chunk with a stick. ''Our illustrious captain has made no secret of the fact he hates the frontier. I wouldn't put it past him to cart the bodies back and report they were slain in a running battle with his patrol.''

''So he gets all the credit and all the glory.''

''Exactly. And none of us are about to dispute him. He could make our lives very miserable if he had a hankering to.''

The situation in Texas was much too confusing for Flavius's liking. What with the Spaniards and the Mexicans and the American settlers all at loggerheads, it was a marvel they were able to get along at all. Then there were the Comanches, who wanted *everyone* out of the territory. Flavius would be the first to admit he wasn't the shrewdest person alive, but even he was smart enough to foresee that a lot of blood would be spilled before it was all said and done.

Davy strolled over and sank onto the log. His legs and backside were sore from having spent practically every waking moment in the saddle. He stretched, and happened to see a large glob of fat ooze from the meat and splat onto a crackling branch.

The sight swept Davy back in time to the Creek War, to that terrible day at Tallusahatchee. The Indians had been unaware a force of nine hundred men, consisting mainly of militia and rangers, had surrounded their town.

The first inkling the Creeks had of impending disaster was

when Captain Hammond's rangers advanced in a skirmish line. Raising war cries, the warriors bounded to the attack— straight into the waiting guns of the whites.

The official report claimed a few women and children had been accidentally slain by overeager soldiers. But Davy had been there. He'd seen Indians of both sexes and all ages shot down on purpose. Shot down like dogs. One, a beautiful young Creek woman, had been literally blown apart by some twenty balls. Others had perished even more horribly.

The official report claimed every last warrior fought to the last with his dying breath. But Davy knew differently. Most had wanted to give up. The warriors had signaled as much— and been ignored. One hundred and eighty-six Creek men died that day, to say nothing of the women and children never officially listed.

But the worst part of the battle, the part that lingered in Davy's memory and gave him nightmares on occasion, came after the fight was over, after the last of the Creeks had been killed.

At one point during the clash, a house with close to fifty Creeks inside had been set ablaze. Reluctant to come out into the withering hail of lead that awaited them, the Creeks had been overcome by smoke and burned to death.

The day after the Battle of Tallusahatchee, someone discovered a cellar under the Creek lodge. A cellar brimming with potatoes.

Davy and most everyone else had been as famished as starving wolves. Provisions had been scarce, the troops subsisting on half rations for days. Eyes agleam, as gaunt as scarecrows, they had ringed the cellar, licking their lips and hungrily eyeing the cache of ripe potatoes. There was enough for all to have a share. But no one wanted to be the first to partake. With good reason.

The potatoes were coated with fat. It lent the illusion they had been stewed in a pot of simmering meat. Which was, in a sense, what had happened. For when those Creek warriors burned, their body fat had dripped into the cellar onto the potatoes.

Davy remembered standing there, staring, his stomach hurting from lack of food and his limbs quaking with anticipation. Hunger and loathing fought for the upper hand, and hunger won—especially after other soldiers began helping themselves, cramming potatoes and Creek body fat into their mouths with relish.

The incident had soured Davy on war for all time. "I wish I may be shot," he had told his wife after his tour of duty was up, "if I'm ever so stupid as to take part in one again."

Seeing the deer fat brought back the sickening memories in a rush, and Davy shuddered.

"You coming down with something, pard?" Flavius asked. Unknown to the others, the Irishman was afflicted with a strange malady that struck without warning and left him as weak as a newborn. What it was, the doctors couldn't say. It had nearly killed Crockett once. So whenever Flavius saw his friend looking peaked, he feared another bout.

"I'm fine," Davy assured him.

Everyone else gathered around. A small sack of coffee had been found in a freebooter's saddlebag earlier. Now Heather put on a pot.

It had been ages since Flavius tasted any. The mere aroma was intoxicating, and he inhaled deeply.

The darkness deepened. A myriad of sparkling stars dotted the firmament. From the northwest wafted a stiff breeze, bearing with it the yips of coyotes and the lonesome wail of a wolf.

Farley Tanner gazed into the night and smiled. "Lord, I love this country. It gets into a man's blood and won't let go.

I could no more go back to Connecticut to live than I could stop breathing.''

Heather looked up from checking the coffeepot. "You're from Connecticut? I didn't know that.''

It was Marcy who answered. "Our folks moved out here when I was knee-high to a calf. They were among the first Americans to put down roots. Applied for a Spanish passport and everything.''

Taylor was doodling in the dirt with his stick. "One day more Americans will live in Texas than either Mexicans or Spaniards. When that happens, Texas will break away and become its own nation or part of the United States. Mark my words.''

Davy swiveled. "Do you really think so?''

"I do. And so does Barragan. You heard him.'' Taylor propped himself on an elbow. "We Americans are a restless breed. We're always on the go, always exploring new horizons. We've pushed steadily westward from the Atlantic since our country was founded, and we'll keep on pushing until we reach the Pacific.''

Flavius tore his eyes from the venison long enough to comment, "The Rockies will stop us. They're too high and too steep for wagons to get across.'' Or so a kinsman had told him.

"We'll find a way. We always do,'' Taylor predicted. "If you don't believe me, just remember what happened in Louisiana. It was under Spanish rule once. Spain passed laws forbidding foreigners to settle there, but did that stop us? I should say not. Over fifty thousand American squatters moved in, and there wasn't a damn thing Spain could do.'' Taylor chortled. "Except cede Louisiana to France after getting Napoleon to promise it would never fall into our hands.''

Davy was familiar with the history. "Three years late, Napoleon broke his word and sold Louisiana to our government for fifteen million dollars.''

"The greedy little rooster,'' Flavius said.

"No, it wasn't greed,'' Taylor said. "Napoleon needed the money to maintain his army.''

Out of the blue Heather Dugan said, "I wish we had a musical instrument. I would love to dance.'' As she said it, she stared at Farley Tanner.

"You'll get your chance, ma'am,'' Taylor said. "Tomorrow night or the next, you and your friends will be the guests of honor at a *fandango*.''

Distracted by the small talk, Davy did not react when one of the horses nickered. But when a second animal whinnied softly, he stood. It was possible they had caught the scent of a prowling cougar—or Comanches. Not venting to needlessly alarm the others, he announced, "Reckon I'll stretch my legs,'' and walked toward the string, Liz cradled in his left arm.

A small figure materialized at his side, limping. "Don't mind company, I hope? Listening to adults talk bores me to death sometimes.''

Davy gently placed a hand on the girl's head. "Don't be so hard on them, sprout. You'll be an adult one day.''

"I don't ever want to grow up,'' Becky said.

"Do tell. Why not?''

"Big people have it rough. My mother, for instance. She's always worried about one thing or another. Sometimes I think all she does is worry. She must like it.''

Davy chose his next words with care. Heather Dugan had cause to be a worrier after all the poor woman had been through. Her early years had been spent under the iron thumb of a vicious stepfather. Later, the man had gone so far as to arrange a fatal accident for her first husband to keep the couple from moving away. The accident had resulted in Becky's limp.

"It isn't that big people like to worry so much. They just don't want the bad things that happened to them to happen to their children."

"Why not just live?" Becky said with typical childish innocence. "What will be, will be, my grandmother always liked to say."

"Your grandma was mighty wise," Davy remarked. Abruptly, he realized fully half of the horses were facing to the northeast, their ears pricked. "Tell you what. Go on back and wait for me. When I'm done, I'd like to hear more about her."

"I don't mind—"

"Please, princess," Davy insisted. He spun her by the shoulders and carefully propelled her toward the fire. "I won't be long."

"Hmmmph," Becky protested. "You're getting as bossy as the others. And here I thought you were different."

Leveling Liz, Davy moved along the string. Whatever had disturbed them was lurking in the woods. He swore he could feel unseen eyes upon him, but whether bestial or human was impossible to gauge.

The fire was to his back, silhouetting him against its rosy glow. Crouching, Davy crab-stepped closer to the animals to make it harder for a human skulker to fix a bead on him. If it was a predator, blending his scent with that of the horses would confuse it. He glanced back just once. Becky was beside her mother, listening to Farley Tanner. None of the rest were aware of the intruder.

Davy's bay was the last in line, which worked out perfectly. It was the one animal that wouldn't shy when he slipped under its belly to probe the murky wall of vegetation beyond. Nothing moved. The wind had momentarily died and the woods were as still as a tomb. Even the coyotes and wolves had fallen silent. Davy could hear the low murmur of Farley's deep voice and the sputtering of flames.

A twig cracked. Not loudly, but enough for Davy to pinpoint the general vicinity of the culprit. Thirty feet away, to his left. Darting into the undergrowth, Davy circled to come up on whoever or whatever it was from behind. His soft-soled moccasins made no more noise than a ghost would on the spongy carpet of grass.

A shape reared up twenty feet off. For a split second Davy saw it, then it was gone, and he was still not sure whether he was dealing with a four-legged or a two legged threat. But he did see that it was circling in a counterclockwise direction and would pass directly between him and the fire.

Pausing beside a willow, Davy braced Liz against the trunk and sighted down the barrel. *Any instant now*, he reflected, and began to ease back the hammer.

Seconds went by. Too many of them. Too late, Davy sensed something behind him, and he pivoted, seeking to bring Liz to bear before he was attacked. Hardly had he started to turn, though, when a steely forearm clamped around his throat and a sandpaper voice snarled in his ear, "Did you really think I'd let you get away with killin' my pards?"

Chapter Three

It was the freebooter who had gotten away!

Even as the realization exploded in Davy Crockett's mind, Davy himself exploded into motion. Tucking at the waist, he pivoted on the balls of his feet. Simultaneously, he let go of Liz, grabbed the freebooter's forearm, and pulled.

The man was caught flat-footed. He grunted as he was flipped up and over, grunted again when he struck the ground. But he was on his feet in a twinkling, the cold steel of his butcher knife glinting dully in the pale starlight.

Davy did not resort to his own knife, snug in a leather sheath on his left hip. He preferred his Creek tomahawk for close-in fighting, and now he whipped it from under his belt on his right side even as he backpedaled to gain room to maneuver.

During the Creek War Davy had learned exactly how deadly a tomahawk could be. During his very first engagement, a muscular warrior had nearly taken his head off at the neck.

Only by a sheer fluke had Davy come out on top. Afterward, Davy had helped himself to the man's weapon, and he had carried it with him ever since.

Now Davy swung, the tomahawk cleaving the air like the stroke of doom itself. The freebooter, though, was no amateur. Skipping to one side, the killer circled and coiled, the butcher knife extended.

Davy adopted a crouch and held the tomahawk close to his chest, ready to slash high or low as was needed. His foe's blade had a longer cutting edge, but the tomahawk was heavier and equally sharp.

The freebooter grinned wickedly and commenced to toss the knife from one hand to the other, slowly at first, then faster and faster. Thanks to the oppressive darkness, it was hard for Davy to keep track of exactly which hand held the knife at any given instant—just as the man intended.

Davy was tempted to call out for help; Flavius and the Texicans would come on the run. But he didn't. In their eagerness to aid him they might be wounded, or worse. And, for all he knew, other freebooters could well be hiding nearby, waiting in ambush.

The cutthroat suddenly hissed like a viper and darted in low and fast. The knife was a blur. Davy countered, the tomahawk deflecting the blade. Sidestepping, he aimed a cut at the freebooter's shoulder, but the man was living lightning. Davy thought he had him dead to rights, but somehow the ruffian dodged.

Thrusting and parrying, they continued to circle, moving farther and farther into the woods, into the darkness. Davy could never look behind him. To do so invited death. As a consequence, he constantly bumped into trees and several times nearly tripped over roots and rocks.

The freebooter grew impatient to end their fight. He bounded in close and hacked at Davy's neck. An upward swing saved Davy from harm, and reversing direction, he sheared the tomahawk at the man's face. The cutthroat jerked to the right, but not quite swiftly enough. Davy felt the blow connect, saw a black gash blossom on the man's cheek. Moist drops spattered his hand as he bounded out of reach.

An oath escaped the freebooter. His other hand shot to his cheek, his fingers becoming as black as the gash. "Bastard!" he hissed. "For that I'm going to carve you into little pieces!"

A blinding whirlwind tore into Davy, a whirlwind of flying steel. The man stabbed, chopped, thrust. Again and again and again. Davy was forced straight backward, always on the defensive, never able to strike out.

Sooner or later the freebooter would connect. It was just a matter of time. To prevent that, Davy had to take the initiative. So when he bumped into another tree, a sapling, he twisted and darted on around the smooth bole. He heard the knife bite into the bark.

Now the tree was between them. When the freebooter lunged to the right, Davy moved to the left. When the man flicked the knife to the left, Davy skipped to the right. It was a stalemate.

The killer didn't like being thwarted. Rumbling deep in his chest, he feinted left and went right. Davy blocked it easily. More frustrated than ever, the freebooter threw caution to the wind and dived, spearing his knife at Davy's legs. It was a reckless gambit. Should it succeed, Davy would be crippled and easy prey. But in order to score, the man had to overextend himself a trifle.

Davy wrenched his feet backward. The knife nicked his buckskins but spared his flesh. As the freebooter started to recoil, Davy drove his right arm down and in. The man looked up, his eyes wide and white and filled with fright. The tomahawk was the last sight they ever beheld, for the next instant the Creek weapon buried itself in the freebooter's temple, opening the man's skull.

The freebooter collapsed onto his stomach. His limbs twitched a few times, the body convulsed violently once, then he was as still as a headstone.

Davy had to use both hands to extract the tomahawk, it was buried so deep. A thick spurting tide pulsed from the gaping cavity to form an inky puddle framing the killer's bearded face.

"Davy? Where'd you get to?"

The shout reminded Davy of his friends. Hastily wiping the tomahawk on the freebooter's homespuns, he wedged it under his belt as he emerged from the vegetation. "Thought I told you to stay by the fire."

"I got worried," Becky said. "You were taking so long."

The Irishman scoured the woods. It was unlikely more cutthroats were out there. They would not have stood idly by while one of their own was slain. So the man had been alone, after all.

"Are you all right?" Becky said.

"I'm breathing, and that counts for something," Davy jested. "Don't go anywhere. I'll be right back." Dashing into the trees, he searched for Liz. Since he couldn't remember exactly where he had dropped her, he had to crisscross the general area. A minute went by. Two.

"Davy? What are you doing in there? Coon hunting?"

It was a private joke of theirs. Ever since Flavius had told her a whopper of a tale about the time Davy allegedly talked a raccoon into shedding its coat to use as Davy's coonskin cap, the girl had been begging him to take her coon hunting so she could see him chat with one.

Davy was about ready to give up and come back into broad daylight when a tiny gleam of metal drew him to his prized rifle. Brushing Liz clean with a sleeve, he rejoined Rebecca

Dugan. She was munching on a piece of meat, her cheeks and chin smeared with grease, the perfect picture of dimpled childhood. "Tasty, is it?" Davy asked.

"You should try some," she said with her mouth crammed. "Before Mr. Harris eats it all. He's on his third helping and the rest of us are still on our first."

That sounded like Flavius. "Lead the way, princess," Davy said.

The others did not ask where Davy had been, and he chose not to enlighten them. They would only fret, probably toss and turn all night, too edgy to sleep. After thanking Marcy for a generous portion of sizzling meat on a stick, Davy lustily bit into his meal. He couldn't count the number of times he'd savored venison, yet this was some of the best ever.

"Taylor's been telling us about the trouble brewing," Flavius revealed. "Believe you me, we don't want to be here when the storm breaks."

"War is always ugly," Taylor commented, a sentiment with which Davy heartily agreed. "And war is bound to come. The Spanish have been lording it over the Mexicans since Hector was a pup, but it's gotten steadily worse over the years. Used to be, the Spaniards treated them fairly, even kindly. Since the empire fell apart, the rulers have grown harsher. More ruthless."

"No one likes to be ground under a boot heel," Farley said.

Another sentiment Davy concurred with. He'd sometimes speculated that if the English had been more tolerant, the American Revolution might never have taken place. His own father had had a part in that great conflict as a frontier ranger.

They made small talk for another hour. Bone weary, the women and Becky turned in. The Tennesseans and the Texicans agreed to take turns standing watch. Farley was first, Davy second.

Flavius relieved the Irishman. As soon as Davy shook him

awake, he stepped to the fire to help himself to another portion of venison. The flames had been allowed to burn low but not out. ''How's it been?'' he sleepily asked.

''Quiet as church when the parson gets up to give his sermon,'' Davy answered, yawning. ''Keep your eyes skinned and your listeners open, though. There's no telling what might be out there.''

''Or who.'' Flavius took a seat on the log and contentedly chewed. His friend soon slumbered peacefully, like everyone else, leaving him alone with his thoughts. And the meat.

A small voice in the recesses of Flavius's mind advised him not to make a pig of himself, but he couldn't help it. The buck had been a big one. Plenty was left over for breakfast. Before the next day was done they would reach San Antonio, so they had no real need to lug a lot along.

He ate to his heart's content, gorging until his belly was swollen and he was fit to burst his britches. Patting his stomach, he stood to limber up. The night air had turned chill and a brisk breeze blew from the north. Angling his rifle, Matilda, across his shoulder, he patrolled the perimeter of the clearing.

The horses were dozing. Off across the prairie something bleated. An owl voiced the eternal query of its kind.

Flavius grinned and wiped his mouth with the back of his hand. Although he would never admit as much to Crockett, he was enjoying their gallivant. He'd met new people, seen new lands, done things he never would have done on his lonesome, things he could brag to his children and his grandchildren about. All thanks to Davy.

Long ago Flavius had settled on the notion that there were two types of people in the world. He called them the ''doers'' and the ''sitters.'' The doers were the ones who bustled about like ants, the ones who saw a thing that needed doing and went out and did it. Tireless founts of energy, they were always doing, doing, doing. Davy was like that. He couldn't sit still for more than a few days without going all squirrelly.

Flavius was a sitter, and he had no regrets about being one. Sitters were content to while away evenings perched in a rocking chair on their porch. Or spend a whole day at a favorite fishing hole, doing nothing but watching the bobber. Sitters had no qualms about letting time pass them by. They saw things that needed doing, same as the doers, but they put off doing them for as long as was humanly possible just so they could loaf that much longer.

Flavius would never have seen the prairie on his own. Or the broad Mississippi. Or the vast herds of buffalo. Or any of the other natural marvels he had witnessed during their trek.

Now he rubbed his belly and turned to treat himself to another nibble. As he did, he heard a rustling noise. A wild animal was moving through the high weeds to the south.

Clutching Matilda, Flavius imitated a tree. Whatever was out there might be harmless. On the other hand, it could be trouble. He strained his ears and heard the swish of grass against a moving form. His mouth went as dry as a desert. It would be just his dumb luck to be attacked by a bear or wolves when he was so close to civilization and safety.

A bush to his left shook slightly. Flavius sighted down Matilda as the branches parted and a dark muzzle poked out. He distinguished a triangular head, peaked ears, and eyes that shone red in the firelight. *A wolf!* he thought, applying his thumb to Matilda's hammer. But looking closer, he discovered he was mistaken. Their nocturnal visitor was a coyote.

"Shucks," Flavius said in relief, and lowered the rifle. Coyotes were harmless, nuisances more than anything else. Normally they fought shy of humans, so this one was being brazen. Casting about for a rock to chuck at it, Flavius was mildly disturbed to see a second coyote off to the right, at the edge of the trees.

"Uppity critters," Flavius grumbled.

Then another lupine specter glided into the open, and another. Alarmed, Flavius retreated toward the fire. He gnawed on his lower lip, debating whether to awaken Davy. But they were only coyotes, and coyotes never attacked people. Not that he had heard tell, anyway.

Most animals were scared of fire. Accordingly, Flavius spied a likely brand and gingerly picked it up. Holding it out from his side, he waved it back and forth while slowly advancing. To his elation, most of the coyotes backed off.

"Scaredy-cats," Flavius taunted.

As silently as the coyotes had appeared, they evaporated into the gloom. But they did something peculiar before they departed. Each and every one glanced around, to the south, as if they heard or saw something out there. At last he understood. The coyotes had not ventured so close of their own accord. Another creature roamed the darkness, a creature the pack was seeking to avoid.

What could it be? Flavius licked his lips and held his breath, but he heard nothing out of the ordinary. He wondered if it was a bear, and wished he had asked one of the Texicans whether grizzlies were found in those parts. He'd seen enough of the fierce silvertips to last a lifetime, thank you.

After a while Flavius decided he was worried over nothing. He gave the brand a hard shake to extinguish the tiny flames, turned, and headed back. After a few steps, his limbs were petrified by the heavy leaden tread of an enormous animal, a beast so immense its breathing was like the raspy wheeze of a bellows.

Every nerve tingling, his knees quaking, Flavius rotated, against his better judgment. He did not know what to expect. A grizzly. A monstrous cat. Certainly not a splendid chocolate-brown stallion fitted with a bridle but no saddle. A stallion lathered with sweat and spotted with grime. The horse bobbed its head and tossed its mane.

42

"Where did you come from, fella?" Flavius blurted in astonishment.

The stallion took a step, then snorted, as skittish as a fox in a henhouse. It was truly a magnificent specimen, its mane lustrous and long, worth ten times as much as any ordinary mount.

Flavius edged forward. "What are you doing out here all alone?" he asked, his voice low and soothing.

The stallion shifted uneasily from side to side. It stared at the other horses, at Becky's feisty mare, and looked about to go over.

"So that's it," Flavius said. "Romantic cuss, are you?" He was two steps away. His fingers rose higher and were on the verge of brushing its neck when the nervous animal danced sideways, refusing to let him get close.

"Suit yourself," Flavius commented. As his beloved wife liked to say, there was more than one way to skin a cat, more than one way to brain a man senseless, and more than one way to get a stubborn critter to do what a person wanted.

Ignoring it, Flavius ambled to the log and roosted. He contrived to sit so he could see the stallion out of the corner of his eye. It watched him a spell, gazed at the sleepers, then cautiously moved toward the string. Several of the animals were awake, studying the newcomer. But it had eyes only for the mare.

What the stallion had in mind was plain. Flavius was glad the womenfolk were asleep. What was about to happen wasn't fit for a female to see, in his opinion. He slid farther down the log so he was between Becky and the horses, in case she woke up.

The mare did not draw away. She and the stallion nuzzled and rubbed each other.

Flavius never had felt comfortable about that sex business. He understood the good Lord had seen fit to create men and women different, and that it was supposed to be normal for a male and a female to know each other, as Scripture phrased relations. But it seemed to him life would be a whole lot easier if men and women were all alike and babies were made by planting seeds.

Matilda liked to snuggle. Often. Always at night, always with the candles out, and always under the covers. But she was a real tigress when her lust was up. Most men would be overjoyed to have a wife like her. Flavius just felt tired a lot, and couldn't wait for the day when she lost interest so he could get a good night's sleep every night.

Now, timing his move just right, Flavius did not rise until the stallion and the mare were so engrossed they wouldn't notice. A coil of rawhide rope on top of the saddlebags was just what the situation called for. Sneaking on over, he slipped a noose over the stallion's neck as neatly as could be.

Only then did Flavius grip the bridle. He counted on the stallion kicking up a fuss, but it allowed him to add it to the string with nary a nicker. Where it came from was a mystery. So was the behavior of the coyotes. They had no cause to be afraid of a horse, unless it was the man smell on the animal.

Flavius ran a hand over the stallion's back. Some of the grime, he discovered, wasn't dirt at all. Closer inspection revealed an awful lot of dried blood. Since the horse bore no wounds, the only logical explanation was that whoever owned it had been mortally stricken. Blood was on both sides and along the left flank.

"So this is why the coyotes wanted nothing to do with you," Flavius observed. He gave the stallion a final pat and moseyed to the log.

The rest of his watch was uneventful. After Ormbach relieved him, Flavius curled up under a blanket. Sleep soon claimed him. At some point he dreamed of returning home, of riding toward his cabin astride the splendid stallion. Golden light bathed the meadow and the sky, and a heavenly choir sang in melodious harmony. From out of the cabin rushed Matilda, radiant in a crisp white dress. She beamed broadly as she raced to meet him, saying his name over and over. Reining up, giddy with joy, Flavius leaned down to kiss her. He never saw the rolling pin that slammed into his head. But moments later, prone on the ground, he gaped dumbly upward and saw her waving it. ''Where in the hell have you been?'' she demanded.

Flavius woke with a start to find he was caked with perspiration. His head hurt where Matilda had hit him. But that couldn't be. It had been a dream.

Dawn was breaking.

Davy Crockett had risen early and dragged the freebooter's body into camp. One by one, as his traveling companions awoke, he had to explain its presence.

Taylor stood over the cutthroat and planted a kick in the ribs. ''Every last one should be exterminated. If they're not, Texas will always be a backwater region where no one is ever safe.''

Flavius related the arrival of the stallion. Having reckoned on being able to keep it, he was mildly upset when Farley Tanner remarked, ''I've seen this animal before somewhere, but I can't rightly recollect where.''

''I think I have, too,'' Taylor said.

''Is it one of Valdez's herd?'' Ormbach asked. To the Tennesseans, he explained, ''Pedro Valdez owns more horses than just about anybody else in these parts. He has a huge rancho outside of San Antonio.''

Brilliant pink streaks heralded the new day as they forked leather and rode out. The freebooter was left in the clearing, covered with stones and branches. ''It's better than the son of a bitch deserves'' was Farley's eulogy.

Davy moved out ahead of the others to act as advance

guard. It had saved their hash once; it might again. Not more than an hour later he came on tilled fields, and soon thereafter saw buildings to the southwest. Starkly somber buildings, eerily black against the morning sky.

Fire had gutted them. A small house, a couple of sheds, a barn, all were in ruins. Charred beams spiked skyward amid piles of rubble. Four freshly dug graves in the front yard disclosed the fate of the owners.

The others raced up when they caught sight of the blackened ruins.

"This must be one of the places the freebooters struck," said Taylor as he slowed. "Old Sanchez owned it. Nicest man you'd ever want to meet. Always willing to share the shirt off his back. Had a wife and two grown sons."

"So the freebooters hit Mexicans as well as Americans?"

Raw hatred turned the Texican's features livid. "They massacre everyone. Young, old. Men, women. Doesn't matter what nationality you are." He uttered a lurid oath. "Not more than four months ago they dashed out a baby's brains against a tree."

Davy did not deem it wise to linger. Pushing on across hilly country, within another hour they came on another homestead. It had suffered the same fate. Burnt buildings were all that remained of a family's loving toil.

All the Texicans were mightily moved, and Davy couldn't blame them. The freebooters were a scourge of vile locusts stripping the land bare. Who could fault the people of Nacogdoches for wanting to pull up stakes and move to healthier climes? But once that happened, what would become of the other two towns, San Antonio and La Bahia?

"This farm belonged to a man named Alverez," Farley Tanner declared, then snapped his fingers and pointed at the brown stallion. "Now I remember where I saw that horse before. It belonged to Alverez's oldest son."

"And we know where he is," Taylor said, bobbing his chin at another batch of recent graves.

While saddened to hear about those who had died, Flavius Harris was secretly pleased no one would dispute him for ownership of the stallion. In the short while he'd ridden the animal, he'd taken quite a shine to it.

Not until the middle of the afternoon did their party crest hills overlooking their destination. "San Antonio," Taylor said proudly. "A hundred years old, if it's a day. Here is where I've put down my roots. Here is where I'll stay until it's time to plant me."

Winding down to a rutted dirt road, they plodded past an abandoned mission, symbol of the widespread religious fervor of the Franciscans, who once boasted a string of such missions from Texas clear to California.

"This was San Antonio de Valero," Taylor said. "In its prime, it was one of the most prosperous ever established. Nowadays, most folks call it the Alamo."

Flavius couldn't wait to ride into town. After weeks in the wild, he was raring for a keg of ale and a haunch of beef. Somehow he'd gotten the impression San Antonio would be a lively little place, maybe as wild and woolly as St. Louis. He could not have been more wrong.

Most of the buildings were arranged in a maze of narrow twisted streets and alleys. The majority of houses had been fashioned from rough logs, the gaps filled in with mud. The populace was generally poor. And the vitality Flavius yearned for was nowhere evident. Instead, San Antonio was a sleepy center where idle groups of townspeople stood around not doing much of anything except maybe listening to roving musicians.

Farley Tanner led them to a broad plaza at the center. Here vendors had set up small stalls to sell paltry wares. Wagons laden with goods were parked at random. Men in wide-brimmed sombreros strolled aimlessly, admiring women in gaily colored dresses.

At a table sat some travelers enjoying food and drink. It reminded Flavius he had not eaten since dawn. Drawing rein, he hungrily appraised plates of Mexican food the likes of which he had never set eyes on before. When a young woman who was dispensing bowls of gooey beans looked up and said a few words in Spanish, Flavius grinned and declared, "If you're asking what I think you're asking, ma'am, I'd have to say yes. I've never been known to refuse a lick of food in my life."

Flavius started to dismount when a shrill outcry to his rear about scared the living daylights out of him. Glancing around, he was stunned to behold an elderly woman barreling toward him, waving a gnarled cane.

"*Ladron! Ladron!*" she screamed. Then, in English, "Thief! Thief! Someone shoot this gringo!"

Chapter Four

Flavius Harris was so dumbfounded that he made no move to protect himself when the old woman lanced her thick cane at his midriff. For someone so wizened and ancient, she was remarkably strong. He was knocked sideways. Frantically, he snatched at the saddle horn, but gravity defeated him. Much to the amusement of many of the onlookers, he was dumped onto his posterior in the plaza dust.

Still screeching, the crone raised the cane for another blow.

Davy Crockett reached them before the cane could descend. Grabbing it and holding fast, he showed more teeth than a patent medicine salesman. "Howdy, ma'am. While I'd be the first to admit my friend can be downright aggravating at times, beating him to death is hardly called for."

Flustered, the woman did not know what to do. She rattled a long sentence in Spanish, then poked a crooked finger at Flavius, then at the brown stallion.

"Sorry, ma'am," Davy said. "My Spanish is as rusty as

my Greek. I can't make a lick of sense of what you're say-ing.''

"I can," Taylor interjected.

He listened while the crone justified her assault. A small crowd gathered. Davy helped Flavius to his feet and they stood shoulder to shoulder, not knowing what to make of all the attention. Whatever Taylor said to the old woman pacified her, and she shuffled off. With the crisis past, singly or in little groups the onlookers went on about their own business.

"So what was that all about?" Davy asked when they were alone again.

Taylor jerked a thumb at the stooped figure blending into the crowd. "Dolores, there, is a second cousin of Alverez, the owner of one of those burned-out ranches we saw. She'd heard about the attack. So when she saw your pard on Alverez's prized horse, she jumped to the conclusion Flavius must be a freebooter.''

"Me?" Flavius squawked.

"Good thing you weren't by yourselves," Taylor com-mented. "These folks would tear a real freebooter limb from limb with their bare hands."

Suddenly queasy, Flavius snagged the stallion's reins. "If that's how they feel, here. Give the horse to the old woman."

"Dolores doesn't want it. She can't ride, what with her legs half crippled by rheumatism. Since Alverez had no other kin I know of, I'd say the animal is yours to keep if you're so inclined."

On the one hand, Flavius was glad. On the other, he worried what might happen if any of Alverez's friends caught him on the stallion.

Farley Tanner pushed his wide-brimmed black hat back. "Now we've got to settle where all of you will be staying. There are rooms to spare out at my ranch. I'll be taking Sis

50

and my mother there directly, and you're welcome to tag along.''

"Or there is the *posada,* the inn, here in town.'' Taylor gestured at a long, low structure across the way. "It's not exactly the St. Louis Imperial, but they're generous with meals and the beds are clean.'' He paused. "I'd invite you to my place, but it's cramped enough with just me.''

Davy weighed their choices. It would be nice to stay with the Tanners. Farley had promised to show him the workings of a big ranch, knowledge that would come in handy one day if Davy ever prevailed on Liz to move to Texas and apply for a grant of their own.

"Becky and I will stay at the inn,'' Heather Dugan announced, surprising everyone.

Farley turned so abruptly, he nearly tripped over his own feet. "What? I won't hear of it. You're all alone, with no kin, no one to look out for you. Marcy and I insist you stay at our ranch.''

"It wouldn't be fitting.''

"Why not? My sister and my mother will be there to act as chaperones. No one can accuse you of improper behavior.'' Farley rested a hand on one of his expensive flintlocks. "At least, no one had better try.''

"You're very gallant,'' Heather said, aglow with something other than gratitude. "But I don't want tongues wagging at my expense. It wouldn't do to have people think I'm a loose woman, not if Becky and I end up settling here.'' She mustered a wan grin. "A woman has her reputation to think of, you know.''

Marcella placed a hand on her brother's shoulder. "I'm afraid Heather has a point. You know how people are. They might not think she's much of a lady.''

Farley glowered at the people lounging about the public square. "I'll kill anyone who claims different.'' Impulsively, he clasped Heather's hand. "Who cares what they think? It ain't right, I say, staying here by your lonesome with no one to look out for you."

Davy Crockett made up his mind. "She won't be alone. Flavius and I will stay at the inn, too. How would that be?"

Uncertainty etched Farley's handsome features. "I don't know . . ."

"It's for the best," Marcy declared.

"And I'll be just a few blocks away," Taylor added. He snapped his fingers at an inspiration. "Say. I'll introduce her to Maria Gomez. They're about the same age, so they should hit it off. And you know how kindly Maria is. She'll take Heather under her wing, make sure she meets all the right people."

Heather draped an arm over her daughter. "I wouldn't want to be a bother to anyone."

"Nonsense, ma'am," Taylor said. "We have to look out for our own. And the sooner everyone in San Antonio learns who you are and who you've taken up with—" Catching himself, he said sheepishly, "I mean, that is, who you might be, well, er . . ."

Farley blushed, Heather turned a pretty shade of pink, and Tanner himself started to resemble a beet. They were saved by Marcy, who shook her head and rolled her eyes. "Men! They don't have the common sense God gave a cactus." Clasping Heather's arm, she said, "Let's get you settled in. Then Farley and I will go find Mother." She steered Heather and Becky toward the inn. "But remember. We insist you join us for supper. No ifs, ands, or buts."

Farley Tanner was still not satisfied. "It ain't right," he protested to no one in particular. Glaring like a bull about to charge, he stomped off.

"Come on," Taylor said to the Tennesseans. "We might as well get the two of you a room, as well."

Davy looked around for Ormbach, but the farmer had disappeared without saying so long. *Probably eager to see his missus and kids again,* Davy reckoned.

Flavius saw a group of Franciscans in brown robes and sandals eyeing them with icy reserve. *What's that all about?* he wondered. Back on the trail, Taylor had mentioned that at one time the Franciscans were a dominant power in the Spanish empire. In Texas alone more than thirty missions had sprouted. Their goal had been to convert the entire heathen world, but in their zeal they had overlooked one small fact. Most tribes were content with the religion they had. Most did not want to convert, and resented being made to adopt new ways at the tip of a lance. Many had revolted, resulting in widespread slaughter. Of the thirty missions that once flourished, only three were left.

A heavyset woman in a gaudy red and yellow dress caught Flavius's eye and winked at him. Stupefied, he did not know what to do. She couldn't be hinting what he thought she was hinting. Women never did that to him.

Taylor had noticed. "You'll find, my friends, that people here are much more open and trusting than those back home. The Mexican people, that is. Most Spaniards are like Capitán Barragan. They distrust us and wish we were gone."

A knot of grungy men loitering at a hitching post caught Davy's attention. "Who are they?" he inquired.

"Never saw them before. Might be just passing through. Or they might be freebooters."

Flavius tore his eyes from the lady who had winked. "You're joshing. Here? In broad daylight?"

Taylor chuckled. "It isn't as if they go around with signs painted on their backs. Sometimes they drift into town claiming to be cattle or horse buyers. Or looking to settle. What they're really up to is scouting likely prospects to raid."

"But we took care of the latest bunch," Flavius reminded him.

"I doubt that was all. Usually there are ten or twenty or more. After they've done their bloody work, they break up into small groups and scatter."

"Well, I hope we don't tangle with any more," Flavius said. Freebooters, Comanches, Sauks, the Sioux, they were all the same to him. They all had one thing in common: They'd *kill* a certain portly Tennessean he was fond of, given half a chance. And he aimed to live to a ripe old age.

A middle-aged couple ran the inn. Their grasp of English was limited, but what they lacked they made up for by being uncommonly gracious and cheerful. Taylor handled the arrangements. Presently Davy and Flavius found themselves occupying rooms on either side of Heather Dugan's. "Figured she'll sleep a lot easier," the Texican said.

Davy opened his possibles bag and checked his poke. Enough money was left to last a couple of weeks if they were frugal and ate only one meal a day. Considering who his roommate was, they'd be flat broke in five or six days.

Taylor paused in the doorway. "You can put that away. Your money is no good here. Farley and I are footing the bill. It's the least we can do after you risked your life for us."

"That's not right," Davy said. He had done no more than they.

Flavius was trying out one of the beds. It was soft enough to float on, softer than his own in Tennessee. The floor had been swept, the walls were clean and white. They had a table and chair all to themselves, and a pitcher of water. What more could they ask for? Afraid Davy would spoil everything, he butted in. "Pay my pard no mind. We'll gladly accept!"

They had the rest of the afternoon to themselves. Heather and Becky were off visiting Maria Gomez, so Davy and Flavius roamed the streets of San Antonio, drinking in the sights.

They were impressed by the easygoing nature of the Mexicans, by the relaxed atmosphere that hung over the quaint town like a shroud.

To the Irishman, it was a tonic. In every city he'd ever visited, the pace of life was as hectic as a rats' nest. People were always skittering hither and yon, getting in each other's way, being gruff or outright mean. In Baltimore, he had actually seen an unwary pedestrian run down in the middle of the street. In Philadelphia it was worse. Folks ran around like a bunch of chickens with their heads chopped off.

Not so here. Davy soaked up the lassitude as a sponge soaks up water. He could not say exactly why, but San Antonio appealed to him as few other places ever had. He would love to bring his family and file a claim, but he was deluding himself if he thought Elizabeth would agree to the notion. She wouldn't cotton to straying very far from her kin. And there were the kids to think of. Some were much too young to make the trek.

Sadly, Davy had to admit it would be a coon's age before he ever set foot in Texas again. If then. But he would keep his visit in mind. And if circumstances were ever favorable, he would do all in his power to return.

For Flavius, their tour of the town reaped a garden of culinary delights. He tasted *enchildas* for the very first time, and *tortillas,* and his personal favorite, *champurrado,* a thick chocolate. He made a mental note to get the recipe before he left, though he doubted Matilda would ever make it. She believed too many sweets were bad for the system. It occurred to him that he might make a batch himself, but he dismissed the notion. Cooking and baking and the like were woman's work.

Shortly after they bent their steps to the inn, they rounded a bend and were face-to-face with several Franciscans. At the forefront, arms folded across his chest, strode a bald friar who wore an immense silver cross that gleamed in the sun like living fire.

Davy drew up short, then dutifully moved aside so the friars could go by. But the bald one was content to stand there scrutinizing them. Davy grew uncomfortable. "If you don't mind, we'd like to be about our business."

In a deep, rich voice, the bald Franciscan said, "You are the new arrivals I have heard about, are you not? The men who slew the freebooters?"

"That'd be us," Flavius admitted. It interested him that all three of the holy men sported stomachs the size of his own, or larger.

"I am delighted to meet you," the Franciscan said, his accent clipped but precise. Offering his callused hand, he revealed, "I am Father Kino, gentlemen. The spiritual welfare of these good people is my abiding passion."

Davy shook hands and made introductions. "We're on our way to the Tanner rancho for the evening," he mentioned.

"Ah, yes. The Tanners. Decent enough people. When they converted, I suspected it was a sham. Merely to acquire their grant, you understand. But Senorita Tanner attends church frequently. And her mother has begun coming often of late."

"What was that about the grant?" Davy asked. No one had said a word to him about strings being attached.

"Those who apply must be willing to convert to the Catholic faith," Father Kino disclosed. "It is one of the main conditions in order to qualify."

"Oh."

Father Kino smiled. "It is not my idea, I can assure you. Faith granted so frivolously seldom is genuine." The friar folded his hands at his waist. "But Spain has always measured her success by the number of souls she has won to Christ. When I was in California, at the mission I founded, in one month alone we won over two hundred souls. What a glorious time that was." Kino's face shone as he raised it to the heavens in devout supplication.

Flavius fidgeted, anxious to be on their way. He had never been much of a churchgoer. Fact was, he inclined to the belief that most men invested in religion at the prodding of their wives. Matilda dragged him to church fairly regular, but it was all he could do to stay awake. He did like church socials, though. Some of the dishes those wives brought were downright divine.

Father Kino regarded the Irishman. "Have you plans to settle in Texas, my son?"

Davy shrugged. Being called that made him feel oddly uncomfortable. Even his own father had never referred to him so formally.

"Most do, once they have seen her beauty. Be assured I would welcome you into the fold with open arms. And never fear. I am not one of those who demand new supplicants attend every Mass and fast on every holy day. I believe in being strict but lenient."

"That's nice," Davy said, for want of anything else.

Father Kino lovingly touched his silver cross. "Well, if you will excuse us, I must not be late for my scourging."

Flavius had been trying to pinpoint the source of a wafting aroma that brought to mind roast chicken, but this got his attention. "Did you say 'scourging'?"

"It is part of my weekly ritual," the friar explained. "Thirty lashes on my back. To atone for the sins of my flock." His smile widened. "Each of us has our own cross to bear, eh?" So saying, Father Kino departed accompanied by his silent companions, their heads bowed.

"Interesting man," Davy said.

"Spooky man," Flavius amended. "Anyone who runs around in a robe and a hood is addlepated enough. But to let himself be whipped?"

"You can't judge another man's bushel by your peck."

Flavius wasn't inclined to debate the point. Every time he argued with Davy, Davy won. But no one would ever be able to convince him that being scourged in the name of the Almighty wasn't stretching Scripture a mite far. As he recollected, the teaching was "love one another," not "whip one another."

Taylor was waiting at the inn, along with rented horses for each of them.

Davy regretted not having time to spruce up, especially after he beheld Heather Dugan and Becky. Both wore new store-bought clothes. Becky was as luscious as peach in a bright green dress and a green ribbon. And her mother was positively beautiful. Attired in a ravishing blue dress that molded to her lush figure like a second skin, Heather was fit to be a queen. She had done up her hair, too, or someone else had, arranging her blond tresses in a golden crown of shiny curls. Davy found himself envying Farley Tanner.

Pleasant coolness replaced the heat of the day as they left San Antonio and trotted westward along a ribbon of a road that had seen a lot of use. They passed poor farm families in simple ox-drawn carts, weary men in tattered clothes trudging home leading burros, lone riders of every stripe—including a handful of lancers. At one point they had to grant the right of way to an immaculate carriage. Through a window a gray-haired man puffing on a fat cigar was visible.

The turnoff was marked by a mound of stones. Taylor swept the verdant land with a wave and said, "All of this belongs to Farley, for as far as you can see. Other men—Moses Austin, for instance—would divide a grant this size up, sell hundreds of small plots, and wind up rich. Not Farley. He aims to make this the grandest rancho in all of Texas."

"Why isn't he married off yet?" Heather Dugan asked. "I

mean, with all he has going for him, it seems strange he doesn't have a wife.''

"It's not from a lack of willing fillies,'' Taylor told her. "Farley is one of the most eligible bachelors in these parts. That is, if you count bathing regular as a habit you'd like your man to have.''

Becky was aghast at the news. "People in Texas don't take baths?''

"Not all of them. Not as often as they should,'' Taylor admitted. "Why, the other day I was downwind from a buffalo hunter who was so ripe, flies that flew near him dropped dead in midair.''

The girl laughed. "No one smells that bad.''

Lights flared to the northwest. Seven or eight buildings were sprawled out over half that many acres. Some were completed, others were in various stages of construction. Out on the prairie Mexicans flailing coiled ropes were ushering about a dozen horses toward a stable and corral. Outlying buildings linked both to a house only half finished yet already enormous enough to house the entire Crockett clan and the Harris clan besides.

Heather seemed awed by the immensity of the spread. "Farley never even hinted at this. Am I to take it the Tanners are wealthy?''

"Let me put it this way, ma'am,'' Taylor responded. "The woman who throws a loop over him won't ever want for spending money.''

Lanterns suspended from trees lit a grassy area in front of the house. Flower beds lent dashes of color here and there. Enormous columns like those Davy had seen at plantations in the Deep South sparkled as if they contained a thousand fireflies. Wherever he looked people were bustling about, cleaning, polishing, preparing.

"All this on my account?'' Heather said, dazzled.

Taylor surveyed the scene and chuckled. "I must admit, I've never seen this place so lit up before. Why, come nightfall, I'll bet you could see it from ten miles out."

Flavius gazed at rolling emerald hills to the north. Lighting up the ranch as if they were celebrating Christmastide did not seem like such a great idea to him. *What if Comanches are out there somewhere?* he mused. But he held his peace. Surely the Texicans knew what was best.

A pair of Mexicans dressed in short jackets, white shirts, and flared pants hastened to take the horses. Both men wore nearly identical *sombreros* and huge spurs with oversized rowels.

"*Caballeros,*" Taylor told the Tennesseans. "Best riders and ropers in all creation. The Tanners have about ten working for them at the moment. As their herds increase, they'll hire on more."

A footpath led to a partially completed front porch. Down the path hurried an elderly woman in fine clothes, her features the spitting image of Marcy's. "Mrs. Tanner. Priscilla," Taylor greeted the matriarch. "You needn't come down here in person. You need to take it easy a spell."

Davy knew what the frontiersman was alluding to. Priscilla Tanner had recently lost her husband of some thirty-odd years. By rights she should be laid up in bed.

"Nonsense. I couldn't wait to meet the young woman my son won't stop talking about."

Heather had halted, and she clutched Becky. She put a hand to her throat to cover some of her exposed skin. "I'm afraid your son has a much higher opinion of me than I deserve."

Davy held back as the mother gave her son's romantic interest a raking probe from head to toe. Heather's happiness hung in the balance, and he was as delighted as she was when Priscilla Tanner warmly embraced her and declared, "If anything, he understated the case. Come. We have refreshments waiting.''

Since the exterior was unfinished, Davy took it for granted the interior would be the same. But apparently, as soon as a room was completed, it was immediately fully furnished. A spacious living room, an ample dining hall, and numerous smaller chambers in the east wing of the sprawling house were lavishly adorned. Polished hardwood floors shone brightly. Draperies and tapestries were in abundance. In the living room was a bona fide marvel: a chandelier. In the corner was another: a grand piano.

''Where did they get all this stuff?'' Flavius exclaimed as Priscilla guided them on a brief tour.

''Traders come from Mexico City every month, and from points east when they can make it past the freebooters,'' Taylor said.

As they entered the living room, Marcy came through a door on the opposite side. Gone was the dirt and dust of the trail, the tangled hair, the shabby dress she had worn when rescued from the Comanches. She waltzed in adorned in the best raiment money could buy, and she was so breathtaking that Davy and Flavius gaped like schoolboys.

Heather Dugan hardly noticed. For right behind Marcy came her brother. Farley wore clothes similar to the *caballeros'*. A wide black leather belt banded his slim waist, accentuating the width of his chest and shoulders. Even Davy had to admit he was as fine a figure of a man as any woman was ever likely to meet. Heather was mesmerized.

Not saying a word, Farley crossed to her and tenderly took her hands in his. As if by magic, the others found something else to do.

Davy ambled toward a double window that opened onto the main porch. A convenient bench in the shadows beckoned. Sinking down with a sigh, he stretched his legs and relaxed, truly relaxed, for the first time since he had struck Texas.

Suddenly two figures came through the opening. Farley had Heather by the hand and led her to one side, within spitting distance of the bench. Enrapt in each other, neither noticed Davy. He was all set to announce his presence when Farley turned and planted a passionate kiss on Heather's mouth.

"Oh," she said when they broke for air.

"I've been counting the seconds since we were separated," Farley said. "You have no idea how much I've missed you."

"It's only been a few hours." Heather tried to make light of his feelings.

Farley did not seem to hear. "Those weeks together out on the prairie. They were wonderful, weren't they? Getting to know you, growing to feel as I do."

"Maybe we should go back in."

"No," Farley said quickly, much too quickly, Davy thought. "I have something to say, and I better say it now while I have the courage."

Grinning, Heather said, "Don't worry. I'll sit by you at supper if you want."

Davy had never seen the tall Texican so deathly serious. It gave him an inkling of what to expect. Sure enough, the very next second Farley Tanner sank onto a knee and held Heather's hand as if it were the most delicate flower in all creation.

"Farley, what on earth—?"

"Heather Dugan," the Texican said, and had to lick his lips to continue. "I would like you to do me the honor of being my wife."

Chapter Five

Before the shocked woman could answer, footsteps drummed on the *portico*. Up rushed a stocky *caballero* who briskly launched into an excited string of Spanish. Farley Tanner had snapped erect and spun. His cheeks darkened, but whether from embarrassment at being caught on his knees or in anger at the message the *caballero* brought was impossible for Davy Crockett to say.

The *caballero* kept jabbing a thick finger to the northwest. Davy looked in that direction and saw nothing out of the ordinary. Over by the stable, though, a commotion had erupted. Grim-faced men in wide-brimmed hats and shiny spurs were hurriedly saddling mounts by lantern light.

"What is it?" Heather asked when the stocky Mexican fell silent.

"Freebooters," Farley said. "On *my* rancho."

"Would they dare attack here?"

"Never," Farley stated with supreme confidence. "They

know how many guns they would face. And say what we will about them, they aren't fools." He hitched at his belt. "We'll finish our talk another time."

Heather snatched his sleeve. "Must you go? Can't your men handle it?"

Farley shrugged her hand off. "Please. What kind of *hombre* do you take me for? I would never ask my *caballeros* to do anything I am unwilling to do myself." Pausing, he softened his tone. "Some of my outriders spotted a large band of strangers about an hour ago. A few shots were fired, but no one was hurt. I must go investigate. That's all."

"What if the freebooters are still in the area?"

"Doubtful," Farley said. "I have more good hands working for me than any American in Texas. It's likely they've ridden eastward to crawl back into their burrows. But I have to be sure."

Heather wanted to say more, but the tall Texican strode off. She started to follow, then stopped, put a hand to her throat, and moaned softly. She did not see Davy rise, and jumped out of her skin when his arm fell across her shoulders.

"He'll be just fine," the Tennessean predicted. "He's a human hurricane when he gets his dander up, as you well know." During their scrape with the Comanches, Farley had proven his courage and ability time and again.

Heather bleakly nodded. "Even so, all it takes is one measly bullet. One lucky shot and. . . ." She didn't finish.

"Tell you what," Davy said earnestly to take her mind off her worries. "Why don't you escort me back inside? If'n we act real friendly, maybe we can set their tongues to wagging. As a lark," he stressed.

Despite herself, Heather Dugan grinned. "I do declare, Mr. Crockett. When you ladle on that southern drawl of yours as thick as you just did, I know we're in the soup."

Her long dress swishing, Heather led the Irishman indoors.

Priscilla was seated in a high-backed chair, chatting with Taylor. The mother's eyes pinched when she noticed her son was missing. Under a huge painting of the gray-haired patriarch of the family, Flavius Harris listened to Marcy relate their grand plans for their land grant.

Being around women always left Flavius tongue-tied. Beautiful ones, like Marcella Tanner, aggravated his condition. He never knew what to say. Consequently, he was sweating torrents and praying to high heaven supper would soon be served.

"Another ten years," Marcy predicted, "and the Tanner ranch will be the talk of Mexico. We'll hold fine balls to rival those of Boston and Philadelphia. When anyone of importance passes through San Antonio, they will make it a point to savor the famous Tanner hospitality."

"That's nice, ma'am." Flavius did not see fit to tell her that balls and such were as foreign to him as talk of life on the moon. He'd never been to a dress ball in all his born days, and wouldn't want to go to one, neither. When it came to dancing, he was plumb hopeless. The few times he'd tried, he'd either trod on Matilda's toes or banged her shins or found some other clever way of making a complete fool of himself. He was so awful, in plain fact, that once, after he had tripped over Matilda's feet and nearly spilled the two of them into a bowl of cider at a church social, she had turned and said in all seriousness that he was a "catastrophe waiting to happen."

Marcy was staring. "You must be the same, Mr. Harris."

"How's that again?" Flavius blurted, realizing he had not been paying attention.

She nodded at the portrait of her father. "He had a wanderlust as deep as the ocean. It's what brought him to Texas. Davy and you must share that urge to roam. Why else have you come so far from home?"

Flavius could have told her the truth. He could have smiled and said, "My pard's to blame, not me. He's the one who

always has to take a gander at what lies over the next rise.''
But for some peculiar reason he puffed out his chest a mite
and announced, "That's us, all right. Gallivanting fiends.''

Just then a servant in a crisp black suit arrived and announced dinner was ready. Flavius hesitated when Marcy held
out her elbow, then gingerly grasped it, much as he would a
brittle egg, and awkwardly ushered her into the dining room.

It was spectacular. A table twice the length of Flavius's
cabin was flanked by polished mahogany chairs. On a flawless
white tablecloth sparkling silverware had been precisely arranged. Fine china fit for Tennessee's governor had been set
out, along with bowls and platters heaped with steaming food.

The sight left Flavius speechless. There was venison, buffalo, and beef. There was ham, lamb, and grouse. Mountains
of potatoes. Bowls of thick gravy. Stacks of freshly baked
bread. Sweet cakes. And more. So much more that Flavius let
go of Marcy and stumbled toward the table as if he were a
dazed sleepwalker.

"Is something wrong?" Marcy asked.

"All this is for us?" Flavius squeaked.

"Well, it is a special occasion," she responded. "My
brother wanted everything to be perfect." Marcy glanced
around. "Where is Farley, anyway?"

Flavius didn't know and didn't care. Forgetting his manners,
he sank into a chair without waiting for the ladies and fondled
the rim of a serving dish laden with thick, juicy slabs of prime
buffalo meat. "Oh Lord," he breathed, inhaling the aroma. It
was sweeter than the fragrance from a bouquet of flowers.

Davy Crockett could not help but chuckle. Priscilla was
regarding Flavius as if he were crazy, and some of the servants
were openly dumbfounded. Flavius had eyes only for the food;
at the moment he was as happy as a flea in a doghouse.

Clearing her throat, Priscilla Tanner moved to the head of
the table and bid everyone to take a chair. She asked about

Farley's absence, frowning when an elderly Mexican whispered in her ear.

Becky finally showed up, watched over by a kindly maid in a frilly apron. "Look what they gave me!" she said, beaming at her mother and holding aloft a large doll similar to those Davy had seen in a shop window in San Antonio that afternoon.

"It was Farley's idea," Marcy said.

Heather bit her lower lip and gazed out the window. Beyond, a veil of darkness shrouded the benighted prairie.

Davy could guess what she was thinking. "Let's dig in before my friend does," he suggested, "or there won't be a lick of food left for us." Everyone laughed except Heather, who was too distraught to do more than politely tweak her rosy lips.

Flavius heard the offhand remark. Had anyone other than the Irishman dared to poke fun at his expense, he'd have taken exception. Ignoring it, he selected a slice of bread and layered it thick with butter, stroking the knife slowly and smoothly, fascinated at how the creamy texture changed with each stroke.

Priscilla asked Taylor to give thanks. The lanky frontiersman bowed his head, clasped his hands, and intoned, "We thank the Almighty for the blessings we daily receive, and for the meal we will partake of. May we find favor in His eyes and be spared from the Evil One. Amen."

Davy cracked an eyelid. He'd never pegged the oldster for a religious sort, yet Taylor was as solemn as a minister at a baptism. "Amen," he chorused when everyone else did, and set to filling his belly.

The women chirped gaily about everything under the sun. Priscilla had been to London, Paris, and Athens, and regaled Heather and Becky with tales of her travels. Somehow the topic shifted to Greek heroes and the subject of Heracles came up. When the matriarch happened to remark that the famed strongman once slew a lion with his bare hands, Flavius looked up from the soup he was inhaling and snorted like a bull.

"That's nothing, ma'am. Davy, here, once killed eight bears in seven days. Ain't a hunter anywhere who can boast the same."

Priscilla took the claim in stride. "A remarkable achievement, I'm sure. But Mr. Crockett relied on his gun. Not his bare hands."

"Begging to differ." Flavius would not give an inch. "But to finish off one of those rascals, Davy had to use his butcher knife and tomahawk. At close quarters."

Becky lit up like a candle. "Did you really?" she asked the Irishman.

Davy swallowed a bite of corn, nodding. They were in the mood for a story, and he aimed not to disappoint them. "It was in the wild Obion country," he said, warming up. "I had a couple of pretty tolerable coon dogs and an old hound that could sing as pretty as you please."

"Dogs can't sing," Becky cut in.

"This one could. Knew 'Rock of Ages' by heart. Anyway, they started a big gang of turkey gobblers and I brought two down. Then, on our way back to camp, I cut through some heavy cane. Along about then that old hound set to warbling. Soon the others joined in. When I caught up, I saw they were after the largest black bear ever seen in America, or I'll eat my coonskin cap."

"Yuck. That would taste terrible."

"The bear was the size of a huge black bull," Davy elaborated. "I just had to have him. So I hung the gobblers in a tree and lit a shuck after the dogs. They were afraid to tangle with the monster, he was so fierce."

"What happened?" Marcy probed.

"Well, they cornered that bruin in a thicket and got into a

pretty considerable snarl. The racket they raised was heard clear down in Florida, I've been told. I couldn't get a clear shot for the life of me. Pretty soon that bear lit out and ran to a high oak tree. The sun had set, and it was hard for me to take a bead. So I snuck closer and saw him sitting in a fork and growling at my dogs.''

''Did you shoot him?'' Priscilla inquired.

''Once. As best I could sight my gun, what with the night black as pitch. Heard him roar, and he came tumbling down on top of my dogs. That old hound yipped, hurt bad. So I did the only thing I could. I drew my butcher and my tomahawk and ran in close to help them.''

Becky was agog. ''Mercy. Weren't you scared?''

''I would have been if I had the brains of a turnip,'' Davy said. ''But all I could think of was saving my dogs. The bear had backed into a gully, so they couldn't get at him all at once. The old hound was torn open, and one of the others was limping.'' He recollected the event as if it were happening then and there. ''I ran up within four or five steps of that bear when he reared and tried to wrap those arms of his around me. I knew if he got ahold of me he'd hug me altogether too close, so I hacked at him with my tomahawk and stabbed with my knife.''

No one interrupted.

''It was a tolerable confusion, I don't mind telling you. There I was, thrusting and slashing. And there were the dogs, biting and barking. As for the bear, he was in a full-tilt rage, and sorely craved to do one of us in. He hurt all three dogs and they drew back. That left just me and him, alone in the black gully, with nary a moon or hardly any starlight to show me where his heart was.''

Becky had her mouth half open, a forkful of ham forgotten.

''I knew it was root hog or die,'' Davy related, ''so I stepped in close enough to have his breath fan my face. Then

I buried my butcher in his chest where I thought his heart ought to be.'' Leaning back, he stopped for dramatic effect. ''That hairy feller straightened up, put his paws to his chest, snarled, 'You got me, darn you!' and keeled over.''

For a bit the room was quiet, then Becky pealed with mirth and the women exchanged amused looks.

''I wish I may be shot if that critter didn't weigh in at over six hundred pounds,'' Davy said. ''Took three grown men and four packhorses to tote the meat and the hide to my cabin. Gave us enough to last through the winter and on into the next spring.''

''You love to hunt, I gather?'' Priscilla asked.

Davy nodded. ''Whatever else I may do in my life, I'll always be a hunter first and foremost. It's in my blood, as folks have it. I've been filling the supper pot since I was old enough to hold a flintlock. Imagine I'll go on using a rifle to my dying day.''

''My husband was a hunter also,'' Priscilla said. ''Walter liked nothing better than to go off into the wilds, just him and his gun.''

Davy had leaned Liz against the table. Patting her, he said fondly, ''Our forefathers had the good sense to include the right to bear arms in the Constitution. I reckon the day we give that right up is the day our country will no longer be called free.''

Priscilla agreed, adding, ''Your passion surprises me. Perhaps you should change your calling. With your flair for storytelling, you'd do well in politics.''

Flavius perked up. ''I've been saying the same thing for years, Mrs. Tanner. Maybe he'll listen to you, since all he does when I bring it up is roll his eyes.''

''I'd sooner be a freebooter than a politician,'' Davy quipped.

''I agree they have a lot in common,'' Priscilla said playfully, "but unlike freebooters, some politicians are honest, decent people. Like you, Mr. Crockett. And the good Lord knows we could use more true leaders in Congress." She made a tepee of her fingers. "If my Walter and I hadn't moved to Texas, he'd have run for office one day."

Davy did not see the link. "What stopped him from running here?"

"Haven't you heard? All top posts in the government are filled by royal officials sent from Spain. Even native-born Mexicans are denied the right to hold office. It's been the same for over three hundred years." Priscilla glanced at the servants. "Quite frankly, Mexico is a powder keg waiting to explode. I have many good Mexican friends, high clergy, *rancheros*, businessmen, officers in the military, you name it, and each and every one of them hates the current state of affairs. All it would take to set them off is the right spark."

"The taxes will be that spark," Marcy said.

Davy looked at her.

"Spain recently raised our taxes so high that—"

A single shot cracked in the night, so loud and distinct they all heard it. Taylor rose and went to a high window that ran half the length of the room. "Mighty odd," he said. "Who'd be shooting this late?"

Priscilla gestured to the elderly Mexican, who hastened off to do her bidding. "I'm sure there is a logical explanation. Let's finish our meal in peace and retire to the library."

Tanner turned. Davy, gazing past the Texican, saw something materialize in the gloom, a vague, grotesque shape that loomed larger by the moment, acquiring the silhouette of a horse and rider, but a horse and rider unlike any Davy ever beheld. For both man and beast were immense, the horse an enormous black stallion whose nostrils and eyes were flared wide, the man a hulking brute from whose broad shoulders flapped a long, coarse cloak.

All of this Davy noted in an instant. They were charging straight at the window, but he expected them to stop short. No sane rider would do otherwise. Grasping Liz, he tried to shout a warning, a shout that died in his throat, smothered by the shock of suddenly seeing the rider's head burst into bright flames.

Demonic laughter rang out. Everyone swiveled toward the source. And the next second the horse smashed into the window at a full gallop, shattering the glass into thousands of tiny shards. Someone screamed. Becky wailed. A servant shrieked in mortal terror.

Davy threw both arms in front of his face to protect himself from flying glass. He glimpsed the giant, roaring lustily and waving a curved sword, a heartbeat before the black stallion rammed into the table. He was knocked backward, off his feet. A chair fell on top of him.

Bedlam ensued. More riders burst into the dining room. Lusty curses mingled with cries of horror. A gun boomed. A gruff voice thundered, "There she is, boys! The old hag! Take her! Quickly now!"

"Mother!" Marcy Tanner screeched.

Throwing the chair off, Davy gripped the edge of the table and heaved upright. Directly across from him was the giant. Flames and smoke spurted from the man's sizzling hair. Their eyes met, and the intruder laughed with abandon.

"Lift a finger against my boys and the women die, landlubber!"

Several servants were sprawled on the floor, one in a spreading scarlet pool. Taylor lay motionless, partially under the table. A pair of scruffy riders had seized Priscilla Tanner and were roughly throwing her over a saddle. She fought like a tigress, but she was helpless to resist.

Marcy was trying to reach her mother's side. Another pair of invaders blocked her, smirking when she struck at their legs and their mounts. "Don't just stand there!" she railed at the Irishman. "Do something!"

But Davy did not move. What else could he do? Eight or nine freebooters were just outside, their rifles leveled. Elsewhere guns crackled and popped. Others were keeping the *caballeros* occupied.

The giant with the flaming hair chortled. "Smart man," he said to Davy. "Odd kind of hat you're wearin', though. Is that a raccoon's butt on your head, mate?"

This from someone whose hair was ablaze? Davy could only marvel at the giant's daring. Pitch had been smeared thick over the man's long locks, then set on fire. So long as the flames were extinguished within a short while, it would do no real harm. A bizarre ruse, worthy of a lunatic.

"Give the lord of the manor a message for me," the giant bellowed. "Tell young Master Tanner his mother is being held by none other than Blackjack Tar. So long as he does as I want, she will come to no harm. But if he defies me, I will send her back in bits and pieces. So help me God."

With that, Blackjack Tar wheeled the black stallion and plunged into the Stygian night. His minions did likewise, the man who held Priscilla giving her a rough smack on the posterior. More shots resounded as the Mexicans tried to stop the marauders.

Davy ran to the ruined window in time to glimpse Tar's flaming head seconds before the flickering orange and red daggers were snuffed out. Darkness swallowed the freebooters just as *caballeros* on horseback lit out after them.

The Tennessean pivoted to help others. He had no inkling of what Marcy Tanner was going to do, so he was caught off guard when she sprang at him and commenced beating on his chest. He tried to clutch her wrists, but she would not be denied.

"How could you let those devils take her? Don't you know

what they'll do? The outrage they'll commit?''

Tears gushed from her eyes. Davy braced himself as she slumped and bawled. Nearby, Taylor was rising and rubbing a nasty welt on his temple. A couple of servants were attending to fallen companions. Davy sought Heather, thinking she could comfort Marcy, and was bewildered to find her gone. Becky was crouched under the table, silently weeping. ''Where's your mother?''

''Those wicked men stole her.''

''*What?*''

Sniffling, the child pointed into the gloom. ''Didn't you see? One of them grabbed her by the hair and pulled her onto his horse.''

Davy had been so preoccupied with their fiery leader that he had failed to keep track of his friends. A check revealed Flavius sprawled beside his chair, crimson matting what little remained of his hair.

''No!'' Davy said, and shoved Marcy into the arms of a Mexican woman dressed all in white. A cook, perhaps. Darting to his friend's side, he knelt. A heavy object had caught the portly backwoodsman across the head, leaving a jagged gash. ''Pard?''

Adrift in a whirling inky current, Flavius Harris grew aware of pressure on his right shoulder. And rhythmic movement. Someone was gently shaking him. Why? What had happened? The last thing he remembered was hearing a tremendous crash and beginning to shift in his chair. Then the ceiling caved in.

''Can you hear me?''

Flavius opened his eyes and experienced a sickening sensation, as if the floor were spinning around and around. ''Davy?'' he croaked.

''Lie still. You took a blow to the head. Hard as your noggin is, you should be fit as a fiddle in no time.''

It was supposed to be a joke, but Flavius did not appreciate the humor. A midget with a hammer was beating on the inside of his skull. "I don't think I can get up yet," he said thickly. "And I sure could use some water."

"Don't move. I'll fetch it."

Many of the plates and bowls and glasses were in fragments on the floor, but Davy found an intact water pitcher and an upended glass. Filling the latter, he was about to bend over when hooves pounded outside.

Toward the house raced a knot of riders led by a madman. But not a madman with flaming hair. Handsome features distorted in panic, Farley Tanner hauled on the reins, hauled so hard his mount's head was wrenched to one side. Springing from the saddle, the Texican took two long strides and vaulted over the windowsill, landing amid broken shards that crunched under his boots. Frantically, he scanned the dining room, his brow knitting in consternation. "Heather?" he cried.

Marcy had been sobbing uncontrollably. At the sound of her brother's voice she tore loose from the cook and flung herself at him. "It was Blackjack Tar! He kidnapped Mother! And Heather!"

"Mother?"

The color drained from Farley's face like water down a spout, leaving him as pale as a sheet. Ashen, he gripped his sister's shoulders. "You must be mistaken. What use would she be to an animal like him?"

Squirming in pain, Marcy exclaimed, "You're hurting me! Let go!"

Davy placed the glass in Flavius's hand and ran to the siblings. In order to help Marcy he pried at Farley's iron fingers, and was in turn seized by the Texican and shaken like a lamb in the grip of a rabid wolf.

"Crockett! She must be wrong. Say she is. Please."

"It's true," Davy confirmed, and quoted Tar's exact message. "I'm sorry," he said. "It happened so fast, there was little I could do."

"It can't be." Farley deflated like a punctured balloon. "Not Mother and Heather, both."

"We'll find them," Davy predicted. "As my grandpa was so fond of saying, where there's a will, there's a way."

Farley Tanner placed both hands flat on the table. "You don't understand. It's not that easy. Blackjack Tar was a pirate once. Sailed out of their base on Galveston Island. The worst of the bunch, he took dozens of captives over the years." Farley hung his head. "Not one was ever returned alive."

Chapter Six

Fully a third of the freebooters had once been pirates or smugglers. As recently as five years before they had virtually controlled the Gulf of Mexico, preying mainly on Spanish galleons.

American ships had not been set upon—initially. It wasn't that the pirates feared the Americans. The truce stemmed from the War of 1812, and the part played in that conflict by a pirate so famous even Davy and Flavius had heard of him.

Jean Laffite was a Frenchman. History might never have noted his existence if not for a tragedy that aroused his undying rage against Spain. In 1797 he had shown up on a Caribbean Island, Martinique, where he had fallen passionately in love with the beautiful ward of a Spanish official. The official refused to let them marry, so they eloped. But their love did not have a happy ending.

The young lovers were hunted down. Their marriage was annulled and Laffite was thrown in prison. In despair, his former bride killed herself. From that day on the Frenchman swore eternal revenge on the Spanish crown. When they made the mistake of releasing him, he launched a career of piracy unrivaled in its annals. And most of his depredations were directed at his avowed enemies.

Along came the War of 1812. By then Jean Laffite was a leader of the notorious Barataria company of cutthroats. The British recognized his ability and offered to make him an officer in the Royal Navy if he would aid them in their war against America.

Unknown to the British, Laffite had a fondness for their enemies. For years Laffite had overseen a lucrative slave-running operation in the southern states. Among his many American friends was a certain hothead from the bayou country by the name of Jim Bowie.

So instead of aiding the British, Laffite rushed to New Orleans to inform the governor of an impending British attack. During the battle, Lafitte's men fought so splendidly they were given an official pardon by the United States government for all past crimes.

In 1817, Laffite set up headquarters on Galveston Island. By 1820, he had virtually swept the Spanish from the Gulf.

In the past few years, though, the pirate leader's fortunes had taken a turn. With the Spanish largely gone, prey became scarce. Some of his men had broken his promise and gone after American shipping. Now pressure was being exerted on the government to drive him from Galveston Island.

With piracy and smuggling largely at a standstill, it was no wonder many pirates and smugglers swelled the ranks of the freebooters roving Texas. To them, the farms and ranches were easy pickings, succulent targets they couldn't resist.

All of this Davy Crockett learned the next morning from Taylor. When the frontiersman concluded his account, Davy said, "I take it you've heard of Blackjack Tar?"

"Who hasn't?" the Texican said glumly. He was despondent over the abductions, but not nearly as crushed as Farley Tanner. The younger man had been all for gathering up every last *caballero* and going out after the brigands, until Taylor pointed out that it might get the women killed. Since midnight Farley had paced the grounds, head bowed, a portrait in misery, refusing to so much as speak to a living soul.

"Where does Tar hail from?" Davy wanted to know.

"England," Taylor said. "He deserted the Royal Navy during the war. Word has it he was an officer. Some say he was about to face a court-martial for brutal treatment of his own men when he jumped ship. At any rate, he became one of Laffite's lieutenants. About six months ago, they had a falling-out over attacking American ships and Laffite kicked him off Galveston Island."

"Why does he set his hair on fire? Is he addlepated?"

"Oh, that. No, he's not a loon. Tar is as canny as a fox, as vicious as a panther. The hair business is an old pirate trick. It's meant to inspire fear in their victims, and it works. Imagine being on a galleon when a horde of bloodthirsty pirates swarm over the side, some with their hair ablaze."

Davy envisioned terrified Spanish passengers quaking in abject terror. "It beats everything I've heard all hollow."

"The freebooters were bad enough before Tar came along," Taylor continued. "But after he joined their ranks and became their leader, they've slaughtered and raided like never before."

"He's the top freebooter?"

The Texican nodded. "Tar is largely the reason the people at Nacogdoches are thinking of calling it quits and abandoning their homes. He murders and plunders at will. And now he has his sights set on San Antonio."

"What do you make of last night?"

"I can't rightly say what he's up to. He's stolen women

before, but only young ones like Heather. For him to take Priscilla makes no sense.''

A soft sound caused Davy to shift. They were on the bench on the front porch. The sun bathed the garden in a radiant glow, but he was in no mood to admire the colorful setting. Especially not when Becky Dugan was six feet away and had overheard every word.

Taylor was equally appalled. ''You shouldn't eavesdrop, child. It shows a lack of manners.''

''I'm sorry,'' the girl said, coming over. ''I didn't mean to.'' She had barely slept a wink all night, crying for hours on end in Marcy's room. ''I just wanted to ask Mr. Crockett when he's going after my mother.''

Davy sat up. He would like nothing more, but he feared bringing harm to Priscilla and Heather.

Becky rested her small hands on his. ''You're one of the best trackers anywhere. You can find my mother and bring her back.''

Taylor came to Davy's rescue. ''Child, there are forty men on this ranch who would go after her right this minute. Think, though. If the freebooters saw us coming, what might they do out of sheer spite?''

Becky pondered a few moments. ''That's if a lot of men go. But one or two could get through. Davy and Flavius. They're from Tennessee. And Tennesseans can do anything. They've told me so.''

Inwardly, the Irishman cringed. His tall tales were catching up with him. How could he explain without making her more miserable than she already was?

''There you are, Rebecca! I thought you were going to wait for me?''

Through the doorway hustled Marcella Tanner. She wore a crisp clean dress and had brushed her hair until it shone, but there was no hiding the dark bags under her eyes or her haggard countenance. "Isabella has breakfast ready. Come along."

Becky held her ground. "Not until Davy gives me his word he'll go after our mothers."

Marcy frowned. "Don't be pestering the men. They have enough to worry about." Taking the girl's elbow, she said, "Now, enough dillydallying. The porridge won't stay hot forever."

From the steps linking the porch to the garden came a low cough. "It's not such a bad notion, you know. Two or three men can pull off what a small army couldn't."

Farley Tanner was a specter in mortal guise. His clothes were rumpled, his hair disheveled. In his right hand was clutched his crumpled hat. Stubble covered his square jaw. His once-wide shoulders were bent under crushing emotional weight, but a faint gleam of hope animated him as he approached.

"I can't stand this waiting around for word from Tar. Who knows what will happen to Mother and Heather in the meantime."

"What do you propose?" Taylor asked.

"The Tennesseans and I will head out within the hour, while the trail is still fairly fresh. We won't rest until we've overtaken the freebooters. By this time tomorrow all of us can be back safe and sound."

"Or all of you could be dead," Marcy said.

Farley gave his sister an acidic glare. "It's our *mother* we're talking about. Would you rather we twiddle our thumbs while those bastards do God knows what to her?"

"How dare you," Marcy countered. "How dare you imply I love Mother less than you?"

"I didn't—" Farley started to respond, but got no further.

"My insides are twisted into a knot, I'm so worried. I didn't sleep a wink. All I want to do is curl into a ball and cry until

I run out of tears. But I won't, Farley. And I won't do what you're doing, either. Wasting myself in useless pacing. Being aloof. Denying comfort to those who need it most."

The blistering rebuke deeply affected her brother. "I'm sorry—" he said, and again was cut off.

"Since you're behaving so childishly, I have to keep my wits for the both of us. I would like nothing better than for Mother and Heather to be back among us, but I'm sensible enough to realize that the risk outweighs the prospect of success."

"Maybe not," Davy said, as much to his surprise as to everyone else's. When they looked at him, he elaborated. "Becky is right about one thing. Flavius and I can track anyone, anywhere. Why, once I tracked a baby turtle through thick grass. Try it sometime yourself." He paused. "Locating Tar's bunch shouldn't pose a problem, but I can't guarantee the outcome when we catch up."

Farley squared his shoulders. "See, Sis? The notion isn't as silly as you make it out to be. It might be the only hope our mother has. Or have you forgotten that Blackjack Tar never leaves a living witness?"

Marcy gnawed on her lip in raw anxiety.

"I have a brainstorm," Taylor threw in. "Give me half your men. We'll follow far enough back that the freebooters can't spot us. That way, if you run into trouble, signal and we'll come on the run."

Davy and the Texicans focused on Marcy. She was the key. Without her consent they wouldn't presume to act. She studied each of them, then looked down when Becky tugged on her dress.

"Please let them. I don't want my mother to die."

The heartfelt appeal did what no amount of argument could. Marcella glumly sighed. "My better judgment tells me we're making a mistake. But I won't buck you, Farley. If you and the others believe it's our only hope, do what you have to."

Brother and sister embraced, Farley smiling and brimming with confidence, Marcy upset beyond measure, fearful of the end result of their decision.

Within an hour the plan was put into motion. The two Tennesseans and Farley Tanner rode northward, their saddlebags crammed with enough jerked beef to last a month. Taylor and twenty heavily armed Mexicans were preparing to leave two hours later.

Marcy and Becky watched from a rear corner of the house, hand in hand. Both waved. Both smiled. But Marcy's eyes misted over, and Becky could not stop shaking.

"If something goes wrong," Farley said quietly, "I won't be able to live with myself."

"We'll do right fine," Flavius said. "I'm just glad I can be of some help." Actually, he would rather swallow burning embers than tangle with the freebooters again. He had been petrified speechless when Crockett imparted the scheme. They were taking an awful chance, not only with the lives of the captives, but with their own.

As Davy had foreseen, the trail was easy enough to follow for the first five or six miles. Thereafter, the freebooters had tried a clever ruse that might have fooled less experienced hunters.

Ripping brush and a few saplings from the ground, the brigands had erased their trail, wiping out every last vestige. But in so doing they left scrapes and gouge marks where the branches and leaves had brushed the ground. Davy was not fooled one tiny bit.

The trail bent to the northeast, into rolling wooded hills, well watered, green and lush. Parts of Texas, Davy observed, were as close to Paradise on earth as anywhere else on the planet. Some rivaled the emerald Eden of Tennessee, which took some powerful doing.

Game was plentiful, but they couldn't risk a shot even though Tar's band was a goodly distance ahead. Some of the freebooters might have been ordered to lag behind, specifically to see if they were being shadowed.

Farley was impatient. He carped about their slow pace so often that finally Davy shifted in the saddle to say, "Enough is enough. Does a prairie dog go bounding into a den of rattlers? Does a doe run in among a pack of wolves? I'm sorry, friend, but Mrs. Crockett didn't raise no stupid children. We do this right or we don't do it at all."

Nightfall found them deep in the hills. From the crest of one of the highest in their vicinity Davy probed the darkness for a telltale pinpoint of light. There was none. Resigned to a cold camp, they munched on jerky, drank some water, and turned in.

Flavius tossed and turned. Not from worry over the women. Or from concern about the impending clash with the cutthroats. He couldn't sleep because his stomach growled like a ravenous bear every few minutes. The jerky had hardly whetted his appetite. It was past midnight when he drifted off and dreamed of being the guest of honor at a sumptuous feast given by the grateful Texicans.

Dawn came much too soon, in Flavius's opinion. Davy shook him awake and he sat up, every joint protesting the hours he had spent on the hard, chill ground. His knees popped when he stood. He longed for a cup of piping-hot coffee. Just one small cup. But Davy refused to make a fire.

"We go without until the womenfolk are safe. No matter how long it takes."

Flavius rubbed his abdomen, which he swore had to be twenty pounds thinner than when their gallivant began. At the rate they were going, within a couple of months he'd be skin and bones.

They pushed on. Farley had brought an item Davy relied

on again and again, a copper-hued spyglass with a magnification factor of ten. They paused regularly to scan to the front and the rear. Once Davy spied slender tendrils of dust marking the progress of Taylor and the *caballeros*. Nearly five miles back, by his reckoning. Exactly as agreed on.

Midday came and went. The temperature climbed. Insects droned in the woods, hawks soared on outstretched wings overhead, sparrows frolicked merrily.

Flavius dozed. He tried to stay awake and alert, but his body turned traitor. As a result, he did not realize Davy had unexpectedly reined up until his brown stallion shied to keep from colliding with Davy's bay.

A couple of miles to the north, smoke wafted skyward.

"A campfire," Farley said.

"Mighty peculiar for the freebooters to pitch camp in the middle of the day," Davy remarked. Not to mention advertising their presence in so obvious a fashion.

"Maybe it's not them," Flavius said. "Maybe it's some hunters or farmers."

"Not likely. There aren't any farms or ranches in this area," Farley responded. "The Comanches are partial to these hills, and no one in their right mind courts running into those red devils."

"Then what in tarnation are *we* doing here?" Flavius almost asked, but refrained.

"Comanches wouldn't make a fire that big," Davy mentioned. Indians always built small ones, as much out of self-preservation as anything else.

Farley hiked his reins. "We all know damn well who it is. What are we jawing for? Every minute we delay, Heather and my mother suffer more."

"Just a moment." Davy drew his tomahawk and nudged his horse to a convenient tree. As he had done a score of times already, he blazed a mark, chopping a crude arrow in the bark to point the way for Taylor.

Hugging the base of the hills, the three men wound to within a quarter-mile of the smoke. In a stand of willows they tied their mounts, then the Tennesseans and the Texican warily advanced on foot.

Rowdy laughter mixed with the hubbub of loud voices caused Davy to question whether they had indeed located the renegades, but there was no denying the evidence of his own eyes. Concealed in rank reeds bordering a creek, he gazed out over a lush meadow carpeted with various flowers.

In the center Blackjack Tar and company had pitched camp. But where Davy figured to find a couple of dozen at most, fully sixty cutthroats had gathered. Their horses were in a long string to the north. Three large canvas tents had been set up, and in front of one a skinned buck roasted over the large fire.

"Who'd have thought they'd be so careless?" Farley whispered.

Certainly not Davy. It made him suspicious. Six sentries roved the perimeter, another three hovered close to the horses, so the freebooters weren't as foolhardy as it seemed.

Farley rose higher than he should. "Where are the women?"

As if in answer, from out of a tent walked Priscilla and Heather, Heather supporting the matriarch. A skinny ruffian who wore a blue bandanna wrapped around his head spread out a blanket for them to sit on. No sooner did they ease onto it than another tent flap parted and out ambled the lord of the freebooters, Blackjack Tar himself. Even from that distance he was gigantic in comparison to everyone else, his flowing black hair and billowing cloak adding to the impression of massive size.

Farley lifted his rifle to take a bead. "There he is! The son of a bitch! I could end his career right here."

"And ours as well," Davy chided, snagging the barrel and pushing it down. "Don't do something we'll all regret. We can't do your mother a lick of good dead."

A whoop at the south end of the meadow heralded the arrival of an additional fifteen freebooters, who were welcomed with boisterous cheers.

"Appears to me Tar is gathering an army," Flavius said morosely. What prayer did the three of them have against so many? For that matter, what use would Taylor and the twenty *caballeros* be?

"They must be up to something," Davy guessed. But what?

Farley hunched forward as if about to burst from hiding. "Look at that son of a bitch! Pawing her like that!"

Blackjack Tar was idly running a brawny hand over Heather's golden hair. She swatted him, eliciting a belly laugh. The words they traded were too far off to be understood, but her meaning was clear.

"I swear," Farley growled. "I'm going to gut that pig and strangle him with his own innards."

The afternoon dragged, every minute weighted by millstones. More freebooters showed up. By sunset Davy estimated over ninety were present—or close to half of the total number of freebooters. Something big was in the air. But what it could be eluded him.

Flavius was a bundle of nerves. Whenever a cutthroat strayed anywhere near the reeds, he tensed in dread.

Farley grew uncommonly quiet, which Davy construed as an omen. The Texican never once tore his eyes from Heather the whole time she was outside the tent. Toward sundown the women were prodded back inside and a pair of guards were posted.

Davy relied on Taylor having enough savvy not to stray too close to the meadow. But along about four o'clock a crackling broke out in the trees to their rear, and he figured the Texican had proven him wrong. Then several wild horses appeared. Apparently the meadow was a favorite grazing site, but they melted into the vegetation on seeing the camp.

More fires were lit once darkness descended. Four does were butchered and skewered on makeshift spits. Kegs of ale and bottles of whiskey were passed around freely. The cutthroats were having a fine old time, secure in their numbers.

"I wish Captain Barragan would wander by right about now," Farley said, breaking his silence. "He might hate Americans, but he's a scrapper. He'd help us lick these coyotes."

Flavius reckoned it would take half the Spanish army and a sizable contingent of Texicans to do the job. The pirates, smugglers, and assorted killers were liable to put up a terrific fight.

"I say we sneak on in while they're enjoying themselves," Farley proposed. "No one will pay much attention."

"You're fooling yourself," Davy said. Hardly any of the freebooters wore buckskins. Fewer than ten had *sombreros*. "We'd stick out like sore thumbs. We'll wait until most of them have gone to sleep."

"Whatever you say."

In the back of Davy's mind it struck him that Farley gave in much too easily, but he gave it no more thought. Much to his regret. For it wasn't an hour later that Flavius tapped him on the shoulder.

"Where did that ornery Texican get to?"

Farley Tanner was gone. Davy had been so intent on the goings-on at the camp that he hadn't noticed. Pushing onto his knees, he surveyed the creek in both directions, then the opposite bank. Between the horse string and the tents a lone figure was rising up out of high grass. "The hothead."

"He'll spoil everything," Flavius said, and scouted the woods for the heaviest growth to retreat into.

The bold Texican pulled his hat brim low and sauntered toward the tent containing the captives. Brashly, he nodded and smiled at some of the freebooters he passed. Most were too busy eating or drinking or joking to pay him much mind.

Flavius held his breath. "I don't believe it. He just might pull it off."

That remained to be seen. Farley was a stone's throw from his goal when a pair of renegades barred his path. One said something. Farley shrugged and started to go around them. The other spoke, and Davy braced for an outcry. Instead, Farley calmly inspected his pockets, then shook his head. Satisfied, the pair drifted elsewhere.

Flavius was gripping his rifle so hard, his knuckles were white. More than anything, he wanted the Texican to succeed. It would spare Davy and him from having to sneak in among the two-legged wolves later.

Farley circled to the side of the tent nearest the creek. It was also the side in shadow. Suddenly ducking, he drew his knife and slashed the canvas from the cross brace to the ground. The two guards, busy talking, never heard. Farley ducked into the interior. Seconds later he reappeared, holding his mother's hand. Priscilla, in turn, held Heather's.

Davy tucked Liz to his shoulder. He would provide what cover he could if they reached the creek.

Farley paused. None of the freebooters were looking toward the tent, but that would change the instant the women appeared. He edged to the corner, and just as he stepped into the open the flap of Blackjack Tar's tent was thrown back and into the firelight waltzed the massive giant.

A bellow was the catalyst for Farley's undoing. The guards whirled and sprang. Priscilla screamed. Farley's rifle spat lead and one of the guards fell, his cranium cored. Letting the long gun drop, Farley palmed his prized fancy pistols. His next shot spun the other guard completely around.

From all directions swarmed freebooters. A thunderous command from Tar to take Farley alive was all that saved the Texican from being riddled or ripped to shreds. They piled on him in droves, overwhelming him by sheer force of numbers. Heather leaped to his defense, but she was seized. It was all over within seconds.

The freebooters parted, revealing Farley in the unyielding grasp of a swarthy quartet. He glared in defiance as Blackjack Tar walked up to him and made a remark that spurred Farley into trying to kick Tar in the groin. Tar, laughing, backhanded the Texican, who slumped with blood oozing from the corner of his mouth. At another gruff command, Farley Tanner was bound and dragged over by the fire.

"Damn," Davy said. "Damn, damn, damn."

Flavius had a more pertinent comment. "What do we do now?"

Chapter Seven

The muted hoot of an owl in the distance. The lonesome wail of a coyote to the south. The low nicker of one of the horses. They were the only sounds to break the stillness that gripped the woodland and the meadow in the middle of the night.

It was close to three A.M. when Davy Crockett waded into the creek and glided along the bank until he was directly opposite the tents. He was well aware of the risk he was taking. Blackjack Tar was no fool.

The camp resembled the aftermath of a battle. Scores of prone forms were scattered at random in slumber. The chorus of snores rose and fell in irregular cadence.

Davy had to contend with eight sentries. Four protected the horses, two roamed the perimeter, and two more were posted at the tent where the captives were being held. It would not have been unusual for some to have dozed off, but none had. All were alert, vastly compounding the danger.

Davy wondered if their vigilance had anything to do with

their leader. Tar had been an officer in the British navy, and the Royal Navy was a stickler for exacting discipline. Maybe Tar ran the same tight ship here, so to speak. Freebooters who neglected their duty might face harsh punishment.

Davy brought his idle musing to an end and concentrated on what he was doing. Now was not the time to let his mind drift. Bending low over the surface, he crossed and carefully climbed onto solid ground.

He was soaked from the waist down. For more than five minutes he crouched in the dark, allowing the excess water to drip off. He also rubbed the soles of his moccasins back and forth to dry them as best he was able.

The sentries near the horses did not pose much of a threat; they were too far off. But the roving perimeter guards were a definite peril. One was coming in his general direction and would pass within twenty yards of the creek. Davy flattened, every nerve tingling.

The burly guard whistled to himself, a bawdy tune popular in taverns from the Atlantic to the Mississippi. Unaccountably, he halted when he was abreast of the Irishman, then turned toward him.

Davy could not believe he had been detected. As dark as it was, the freebooter would need eyes equal to an eagle's to spot him. Still, he tensed, his right hand sliding to the tomahawk at his hip.

The man yawned and stretched. He started to go on, but stopped again to gaze at the creek and smack his lips. Uttering a grunt, he walked forward to slake his thirst.

Davy wished he could melt into the ground. Snaking the tomahawk loose, he removed his coonskin cap with his left hand and held it close to his side, ready to throw.

The guard came blithely on, still whistling, his rifle propped on his shoulder instead of at the ready.

When the man was six feet away, Davy flipped his cap to

the left in a high looping arc. Instantly the freebooter stopped, blurting, "What in the hell?" and pivoted toward the cap. It put him broadside to Davy, just as Davy had planned.

Heaving erect, the Tennessean took a long leap and brought the tomahawk sweeping down onto the crown of the freebooter's head. The keen edge sheared through hair, flesh, and bone as if they were made of wax.

In the process of leveling his weapon, the burly renegade was transformed into marble for a span of seconds, then broke out in violent convulsions. Eyes blank, mouth agape, he sank earthward.

The guards at the tent had not heard. The other roving sentry was across the meadow. Davy wiped his tomahawk clean on the dead man's shirt, then slid it under his belt and reclaimed Liz. He helped himself to the pair of pistols the freebooter had, wedging them close to his own. It made him a walking armory, but he might need an extra gun or two before the night's work was done.

Rising, Davy padded closer to the tents, flitting past sleeper after sleeper. Several times he froze when one of the freebooters stirred or mumbled.

The fire had burned low but not yet out. Davy veered to the right, never taking his eyes off the pair of ruffians who might spoil everything if he made a single mistake. When the tent in which his friends had been placed was between him and the guards, he crept to the canvas.

No effort had been made to sew up the rent made by Farley Tanner. Davy parted the edge with Liz's muzzle and peered inside. It took a few seconds for his eyes to adjust.

The tall Texican was on his side, facing away from the tear. The women were at either end, also on their sides, also facing away. Davy was surprised they were sleeping but blamed it on exhaustion. Moving quickly to Farley, he dropped onto a knee and leaned down to cut the ropes that bound Farley's wrists. Only then did he see the gag. A gag that had not been there when Farley was carted in earlier.

Straightening, Davy peered at Heather, then Priscilla. Both had been tied and gagged. The implication hit him a heartbeat before the interior flooded with light. The front flap and the rent were parted wide, exposing a slew of wickedly gleeful faces.

Prominent among them was Blackjack Tar's. Entering, he held his torch out and scrutinized the Tennessean. "Well, well, well. What have we here, mates? Didn't I tell you we could expect more company to come calling?"

Guttural laughter greeted the jest. Davy made no attempt to use his rifle, not when he was covered by six or seven others and a few pistols besides.

Tar chuckled. "I remember you, Yank. You're the fellow who wears a raccoon butt on his head. Why any grown man would do such a thing is a mystery. But then, you Americans are a crazy lot. At least it's not a skunk butt." The giant cackled at his own wit.

The freebooter with the blue bandanna on his head stepped past Tar, then gestured. Four cutthroats converged to deprive Davy of every weapon and hauled him upright. One removed his coonskin cap, sniffed it, made a show of scrunching up his face, then shoved it back onto Davy's head. Tar laughed lustily in appreciation.

Farley Tanner, Heather, and Priscilla had all twisted and were gazing at the Irishman in regret and sorrow. Davy smiled at each of them in turn to show there were no hard feelings. He had figured he was walking into a trap, but he had to do it. As his grandpa had impressed on him time and again, "Always be sure you are right, then go ahead." No matter what the personal consequences might be.

"So, mate. What might your name be?" Blackjack Tar asked.

Davy told him.

"And how do you figure into this?"

"I'm a friend of the Tanner family. Anyone who harms them answers to me."

The giant's expansive visage split in a grin. "You *really* are balmy, aren't you? Here you are, unarmed, defenseless, surrounded by blighters who would like nothing better than to split you from stem to stern, and you have the nerve to *threaten* us?"

"Let's kill him now and be done with the ass," suggested the man in the blue bandanna.

"Now, now, Mr. Quint. This fellow went to so much trouble to partake of our hospitality, it wouldn't be sporting to deprive him."

"I don't like him, Cap'n," Quint bluntly declared. "Me instincts tell me he's trouble. And me instincts ain't ever been wrong."

"True. But what can he do? He's just one man." Blackjack Tar clapped his subordinate on the back. "You fret too much, mate. Always have. All those years sailing with me should have taught you that I always know what's best."

"Aye, Cap'n."

"Then tie him up and leave him be. He'll keep until morning." Tar turned to depart. "Oh. And remove all their gags. No need we can't be civil and permit them to spend their last hours pleasantly. Always be a true gentleman, eh?" He chortled at some private joke and stalked out.

The freebooters obeyed their leader's orders to the letter. Davy was deposited close to Heather, his wrists and ankles bound so securely that the circulation to his limbs was impaired. None of the other captives spoke until the last of the cutthroats had left.

"I'm sorry, Crockett," Farley said. "Tar threatened to harm the women if I tried to warn you."

"And he promised to hurt Farley if we did anything," Heather said.

Davy tested the loops binding his wrists. As tight as they were, he felt that with considerable wriggling he might loosen them a trifle. He set to it, gritting his teeth against the discomfort.

"The man is a brute," Priscilla remarked spitefully. "A monster who delights in terrorizing others. He should be hung from the highest tree. If my Walter were alive, he would have Tar staked out over an anthill."

"Have you learned why he abducted you?" Davy asked.

"No," Farley said. "He keeps hinting, but he won't come right out and say." Lowering his voice, he whispered, "What about your partner and my men? Where are they?"

Davy hesitated. As much as he would like to disclose the plan his capture had set in motion, he was leery of listening ears outside. "Probably right where they're supposed to be," he said, and let it go at that.

"Tar is up to something," Farley said. "Something big. He's gathering as many freebooters as he can. More than have ever banded together before."

"I shudder to think what they intend to do," Heather said. "An army of men who live to pillage, rape, and murder."

Farley jerked around. "Don't say that word."

"What word? Rape?"

"It isn't fitting for a lady."

Heather bestowed a sweet smile on him. "I like being placed on a pedestal. But we have to be practical. You've seen how some of those men look at me."

Farley's features grew flinty. "If anyone so much as lays a fingers on you, I'll rip out their throats with my bare teeth. So help me God."

Lowering her head, Heather snaked toward the Texican. He pumped his shoulders, levering his body closer to meet her halfway. They ended up face-to-face, nose-to-nose. Farley swooped his mouth to hers to plant a lingering, hungry kiss, heedless of his mother and the Irishman.

Priscilla did not take umbrage. To the contrary, her eyes grew slick with moisture and she had to clear her throat to say, "Look at them, Mr. Crockett. Lovebirds. Just like Walter and I when we were their age." She coughed. "It's unfortunate they'll never know the same happiness Walter and I shared."

"Don't give up yet," Davy said. "I admit our prospects aren't worth crowing about, but we're not licked until we give up the ghost."

"An optimist, I see," Priscilla said, not unkindly.

"What does always looking at the dark side get you, except a sour stomach?" Davy responded. "There are plenty of woes to go around without adding to them."

Priscilla rested her cheek on the earth. "Once I thought hope should always spring eternal. Now I can't help but wonder if maybe that's an immature outlook."

"Not in my book." Davy's right wrist was bleeding, his skin scraped raw by the constant friction. "You can hang me for a chipmunk if I ever give up without a tussle." He resorted to his favorite tactic to take her mind off their fix. "I had a cousin once. The practical sort. Whenever misfortune laid him low, he'd always say, 'That's the way the hog bladder bounces.' Well, one day he was in the hog pen, feeding them, and an old boar went berserk. Slammed my cousin into the fence and busted his neck against a rail. Seems to me that's life in a nutshell."

"How do you mean?"

"It's too ridiculous for words. But we've still got to slop the hogs."

Priscilla began to laugh, caught herself, then broke into racking howls of mirth, so loud that in another minute Quint and two other men dashed inside with pistols drawn. Bewildered, they regarded Priscilla as if she were a raving lunatic. "What's gotten into the old hag?" the sea dog demanded. "Doesn't she know her hours are numbered?"

"So are yours, friend," Davy said.

"Reckon so, do you?" Quint snapped. "Me and me mates will teach you different once the Cap'n is done with you. I'll do you me own self, with this." He patted a dirk on his hip. "Carve you up so your own mother wouldn't recognize you."

Sniffing in contempt, Quint pushed through the flap, his cronies in tow.

"What I wouldn't give to get my hands on that one," Farley Tanner stated.

Heather pecked his chin. "Don't think about him. Don't think about any of those riffraff. Lie close to me and let's savor the short span we have left."

Gazing tenderly at her, Farley replied, "My only regret is bringing this down on your head. If I hadn't invited you to my ranch . . ." Despondent, he closed his eyes and groaned in torment.

"Don't you dare blame yourself," Heather scolded. "Why must men always heap the blame for all the calamity that befalls them on their own shoulders? Blackjack Tar is responsible. Him, and him alone." She kissed Farley, but he did not react. "Damn it! Quit behaving so childishly. I expect better of the man I want to marry."

Farley's head shot up as if he had been booted in the ear. Amazement transfixed him, to be replaced by a flood of affection he expressed by lavishing hot kisses on the woman he cherished.

Davy politely took an interest in a support pole. Both his wrists were bleeding now, but it couldn't be helped. He continued to move them back and forth, up and down, around and around. By gradual degrees he gained a little more freedom of movement as time went on. But it was nowhere near enough. By sunrise he would be no better off.

Priscilla Tanner was resting, her eyes closed. Farley and Heather lay still, glued to each other, salvaging happiness from the dregs of despair. Davy hated to intrude, but he sat up and said, "We should give these ropes a try. Who wants to go first?"

Farley shook himself. "I will. Turn around."

Back to back, the Tennessean and the Texan pried and picked and clawed at the thick knots. They might as well have attempted to unravel strands of steel. The freebooters knew their business too well.

Davy did not give up until an hour later. His fingertips were badly bruised and one of his nails had broken off, but all he had to show for it was a partially untangled knot. One lousy knot. "It's useless," he conceded.

Farley persisted a while longer. The frequent longing looks he cast at Heather Dugan explained why. Yet in due course he sagged, dejected, beaten. "I can't believe it will end like this. Trussed up like a calf for the slaughter."

Davy shared those sentiments. In his younger days, before the Creek War, when, like many a young man, he had dreamed of earning distinction in bloody battle. He'd sometimes entertained the idea he would go down in a blaze of glory, dying amid a heap of fallen foes. Now he would much rather die peaceably in his sleep. But both were to be denied him unless his ruse worked.

Dawn was not far off. A few chirping birds signaled its advent, and before long a commotion outside indicated some of the freebooters were up and about. Pots and pans clanged. The fire crackled noisily.

Farley lay beside Heather, their cheeks touching. "I'm so sorry, dearest," he said softly.

"The only thing I regret," she responded, "is having our love nipped in the bud."

From the large tent across the way issued a rumbling bellow. "Quint? Mr. Quint? Where the hell is my coffee?"

It wouldn't be long, Davy mused. Sliding to the cut canvas, he poked his head out. To the east the sky had acquired a pink tinge. Cutthroats were engaged in a variety of task: making breakfast, loading guns, sharpening cutlasses and swords and knives, and dressing. Most were suffering from lingering aftereffects of their debauch the evening before, testified to by the empty bottles and kegs strewn everywhere.

Davy was more interested in the reeds lining the creek. At a certain spot adjacent to a lightning-scarred tree they parted and Flavius briefly showed himself. Davy nodded, then drew back before any of the freebooters caught on.

"What in blazes do you have to smile about?" Farley inquired.

"We're still alive, aren't we?" Davy replied.

"Small comfort. We'll never see another morning."

As if to accent the point, eight members of the brigand fraternity arrived. Two seized each captive and dragged them outdoors, over to where a log had been positioned close to the fire. They were rudely dumped and left to their own devices for the next twenty minutes, until in the growing light of the new day came Blackjack Tar, dressed as usual in his flowing cloak and holding a cup of steaming coffee.

"Morning to you, ladies," the Britisher said. "I do hope you were able to get some rest despite the deplorable accommodations."

Heather faced him squarely. "Go to hell."

Sighing, Blackjack Tar nodded at his right-hand man. "See, Mr. Quint? You try to do the right thing and you're treated with scorn. I'd be grateful for an extra few hours of life, were it me." Taking a loud sip, he licked his lips, then soberly surveyed his prisoners. "Were we on the high seas I'd have each of you walk the plank. As it is, I'll have to make do with a bullet in the brain."

Priscilla stirred. "Do your worst, you beast. The people of Texas will hunt you down one of these days and make you pay for your filthy crimes."

"I doubt it, granny. The Royal Navy couldn't make me toe the line. Neither could Jean Laffite. And the pathetic rabble who call this godforsaken country home can't hold a candle to either." Tar swallowed more coffee. "Besides, another week and I'll be shut of Texas for good."

"You're giving up your piratical ways?" Priscilla said.

The giant snorted. "Not in this life. I'll be leaving for greener pastures, as the old saw goes. Have to. There won't be much of anything left here worth my bother."

Davy grew interested. He scanned the dozens of unkempt figures milling about the meadow and put two and two together. "You're planning one last big raid. All or nothing. Is that it?"

"Give the lad sixpence," Tar cracked. "In another six months Nacogdoches will be an empty shell. La Bahia has little to offer. That leaves San Antonio and the surrounding *ranchos*. Plum enough pickings, in one fell swoop. Then I can move on to bigger and better bounty."

Farley Tanner sat up. "My ears can't be working properly. I'd swear you're about to attack San Antonio."

Blackjack Tar smirked at Quint. "And you told me Texicans are dumber than buffalo. This one is catching on."

"I hope you try, you bastard," Farley said, squirming onto his knees. "I honestly do. It will be the last plundering you ever do. Over eight hundred people live in and around the town. They'll rise up and crush these no-account scum."

"Think so, do you?" the giant responded sarcastically. "But there are a few flaws in your logic, Yank. In the first place, only about six hundred actually live in the town. Of those, over half are women and children. Another third are older men who spend their days sitting in the sun dreaming of their youth.'' Tar paused. ''When all is said and done, there are only about a hundred and fifty able-bodied fighters. And by this time tomorrow I'll have one hundred and twenty freebooters at my disposal.''

''You'll never pull it off,'' Farley insisted, but he sounded less confident than he had previously.

''Strategy, Yank, is everything. What do you reckon will happen if we hit San Antonio at daybreak, when most everyone is either asleep or too groggy to see straight? I'll tell you. We'll sow panic that will spread like wildfire. Most everyone who can will flee to the south. What little resistance we encounter will be easily crushed. Leaving us to take what we want, do what we want.''

Farley grasped at straws. ''The Spanish army will send troops.''

''Oh, please. Barragan's pitiful handful pose no threat. As for reinforcement, they won't arrive for weeks. By then my mates and me will be long gone, to a ship waiting for us on the coast. Then it's off to the Caribbean and doing what I do best.''

''Being a pirate.'' Priscilla reeked contempt.

''Exactly, old crock. And damn proud of it.'' Tar rested his elbows on his sturdy thighs and fingered the rim of his dented tin cup. ''You're quick to judge, lady. But tell me where I'm different from any politician or rich landowner you know.''

Priscilla was so mad, she quivered like an agitated leaf. ''They don't steal or kill or destroy what isn't theirs!''

''No? And what do you call taxes, if not a legal means of stealing from the poor to give to the rich?''

''Utter nonsense.''

''Is it? And I suppose it's nonsense the Spanish crown destroys anyone who dares oppose their rule? Or that in my own country, merry old England, the royals have used their subjects as cannon fodder to wipe out their enemies?'' Tar shook his great head. ''No, granny. If you were honest, you'd admit I am no different from those who have set themselves up as our lords and masters. Except I don't hide behind laws and regulations and the like.''

Farley would not let his mother get the worst of it. ''Sugarcoat your actions all you want. It won't change the facts. You've butchered innocents. You deserve the same fate.''

''No argument there, Yank,'' the giant admitted. ''But you'll have to excuse me if I don't stick my head into the noose anytime soon.'' Guffawing, Tar placed the cup on the log, then rose. ''Enough chat. Any last words before we get to it?''

''There's one thing I'd like to know. Why did you kidnap my mother and Heather?'' Farley asked.

Blackjack Tar shrugged. ''It seemed the smart thing to do. You have over three dozen tough Mexicans at your beck and call. Enough to cause me headaches if you weren't kept from interfering.'' He grinned. ''I was going to send a rider advising you to stay put at your ranch until I was through in San Antonio. But you've saved me the trouble. Without you to lead them, your men aren't half the threat they'd be otherwise.''

''You're wrong,'' Farley declared, but everyone there knew the freebooter had the situation pegged.

''So. Anyone else have any last words?'' Tar wondered.

''I do,'' Davy said.

''Let's hear them, raccoon-head.''

''I'd like you to surrender.''

Blackjack Tar blinked. The hilarity that ensued shook his titanic frame from top to bottom. Slapping his sides, he tried to reply but couldn't form a coherent sentence. Whatever else might be said about the man, there was no denying he had a

103

marvelous sense of humor. Some of the freebooters joined in. Others, Quint among them, eyed the Tennessean with bloodthirsty interest.

"Surrender, is it?" Tar said, controlling himself. "Lord, I like you, lad. It's too bad we didn't meet under different circumstances. A few drinks under our belts, and I'd wager you could keep me in stitches for hours. Now, any last words? Seriously."

"I was serious."

"Is that so? And if I don't?"

Davy slowly rose into a squat. "In that case, I'm afraid I'll have to kill you."

No one laughed. No one grinned. Blackjack Tar chewed on his mustache, his beetling forehead furrowed. "Damned if part of me doesn't believe you. But the other part says you're bluffing, mate. So I'm calling your bluff." Sliding the cutlass from its scabbard, Tar elevated it for a lethal stroke.

Chapter Eight

Davy Crockett never so much as flinched. Bound and helpless, partially hemmed in by coldhearted butchers who wouldn't think twice about making worm food of him, he showed no fear. As the giant called Blackjack Tar elevated the cutlass to cleave Davy's skull in half, Davy calmly looked up, straight into Tar's dark eyes, and said in an even tone, "I wouldn't, were I you, hoss. Not unless you're bulletproof."

The Englishman was poised for a fatal slash. Every iron muscle on his neck and wrist bulged. Another second, and the deed would be done. But he met Davy's stare, met it and paused, hesitating so long that murmurs broke out among the freebooters. "Bold words, raccoon-head," he said at last, "but you're not holding a gun."

"It's not me you need to worry about."

"Oh?" Tar lowered his arm a trifle. "Then who is going to fill me with lead?"

"They are," Davy said, and nodded toward the creek and

the high reeds that framed it. Simultaneously, he pumped his arms several times in the agreed-upon signal. Immediately, Flavius and Taylor and the twenty Mexicans rose in a row, rifles tucked to their shoulders. Every last muzzle was trained unerringly on the gigantic form of Blackjack Tar.

The freebooters cursed and shouted in alarm, raising their own weapons. Some started to rush toward the creek but were halted in midstride by a roar from their enormous leader. Although some of the cutthroats were between Tar and the creek and in the line of fire, he was so huge, so massive a target, that the riflemen in the reeds were certain to put enough balls into him to slay him instantly.

Tar realized that, even if many of his men did not. "No one move!" he shouted. "No one shoot! Anyone who does will answer to me! And by the queen's garters, I'll have your head on a platter!"

The freebooters did not like being held at bay. They grumbled, they nervously shifted, they flexed fingers on their weapons. But such was the power Tar had over them that not one renegade opened fire.

The giant grinned down at Davy and jabbed his cutlass at the Texicans. "Your idea, I take it?"

Davy nodded.

"Arranged before you even snuck into camp, I'd guess?"

Davy smiled.

"Set up just in case you were caught?" Tar chuckled. "A tactic worthy of me. But how did you know I wouldn't kill you on the spot last night? Say, in the tent?"

"I met an actor once, in Memphis. About talked my ear off over his cups. Went on and on about how every thespian should have a flair for the dramatic," Davy related. "You have the same flair. You're part showman, Tar. The way you set your hair on fire. That cloak. How you like to swagger about. I reckoned you'd want to make a show of our deaths. And I was right.''

"You took an awful gamble. I admire that.'' Tar lowered the cutlass to his side. ''There's more to you than I suspected, lad. I underestimated you. I won't make the same mistake twice.''

"You won't get the chance.'' Davy raised his wrists. ''Untie me. Untie all of us. And be quick about it. All I have to do is call out and twenty-two slugs will rip through you before you can bat an eye.'' He had the giant dead to rights. He read it in Tar's expression. But someone saw fit to butt in.

"Don't do it, Cap'n,'' Quint angrily interjected. ''Drop down flat, so they can't hit you, and me and the boys will rush those blighters in the cane.''

The idea appealed to Tar. Davy could tell. ''Do you honestly think you're faster than a bullet?'' he asked. ''A *swarm* of bullets?''

Tar chewed on his mustache and glanced at the Texicans. Taylor picked that moment to holler, ''Free your captives now or else there will be hell to pay!'' The faces of the men holding the rifles were set in firm resolve, the rifles themselves as steady as rock.

"Cut them loose, Mr. Quint.''

Quint growled and gestured. ''I'll be damned if I will, Cap'n! We can't let a bunch of scurvy buggers tell us what to do. It ain't our way. We're the free company! Let's show them what for!''

The giant's eyes glittered like the tips of twin rapiers. ''I will only say this once more, Mr. Quint. And count your lucky stars that we go back a long way together, or I would personally separate that stupid head of yours from your shoulders.'' He leaned toward his lieutenant. *''Cut them free.''*

The sea dog barked instructions. Men rushed to obey, then moved back again. Davy tried to stand, but his legs lanced with pain. The blood flow had been cut off for too long. He had to get them working again quickly.

Every second of delay was critical. Some of the freebooters were fidgeting and eyeing the Texicans as if inclined to disobey Tar. All it would take was one careless cutthroat to start a bloodbath.

His jaw clenched, Davy slowly rose. Wobbly, he shuffled in a small circle, lifting each leg high in turn. Heather also stood, but Farley and Priscilla were still on their knees. "Our weapons, Tar. All of them."

The Englishman issued commands. Muttering oaths and protests, freebooters brought the guns and knives and tomahawk. They even brought the two extra pistols Davy had taken from the slain sentry, pistols he passed out to each of the women. Holding Liz again filled him with renewed confidence. Pointing her at the giant, he said, "Shuck your pigsticker and your flintlocks. You're coming with us."

A hush fell over the band. Blackjack Tar become the center of attention. What the giant did next, Davy knew, would determine whether he and his friends lived or died.

"Where do you think you're taking me, Yank?"

Davy told the truth. "To San Antonio to turn you over to the Spanish authorities."

Many of the freebooters snickered or chortled, but Blackjack Tar wasn't one of them. "Overstepping yourself, aren't you, Crockett? Your piddling bunch is going to take me all that distance? With my boys dogging your heels every step of the way?"

"Your men won't give us a lick of trouble."

"And why is that?"

Davy hiked Liz so the barrel was inches from the Englishman's face. "Because if I so much as see a blade of grass move when it shouldn't, I'll send you into the Hereafter."

Quint cursed. "He's bluffin', Cap'n. He knows that if he

kills you, we'll skewer these landlubbers like pigs on a spit."

Tar was undecided. Davy needed to shift the scales in his favor, so he declared, "When a man has nothing to lose, he'll risk losing everything. I reckon you're as aware of that as I am."

"Say the word, Cap'n," Quint goaded. "Just one word. In another minute this upstart will be a bloody smear on the grass."

The outcome hung in the balance. Then a rifle cracked, over in the reeds. Taylor's gun spewed lead and smoke and a hornet buzzed past the giant's head. "What's the delay over there?" Taylor shouted. "Quit stalling, Tar, or the next shot will be between your eyes! Let the captives go!"

A flush of resentment was the only emotion Tar betrayed as he dropped his cutlass and unlimbered his brace of pistols. "You've won for now, coon butt," he said to Davy, "but I wouldn't give odds on my reaching San Antonio. It's a long way off through rugged country. Anything can happen."

Davy moved around behind Tar and jammed Liz against his spine. "Start walking. Keep your hands out from your side where I can see them at all times. And whatever you do, don't trip. My rifle has a hair trigger."

Glancing once at Quint, Blackjack Tar obeyed, smiling jauntily and strolling along as if he did not have a care in creation. Several freebooters moved to intervene, but he stopped them with a flick of a finger. "In due time, mates," he said. "All in due time."

Farley brought up the rear to protect the women. It was as plain as the nose on his face he was eager to shoot someone— anyone at all. None of the freebooters tempted fate, though.

The skin between Davy's shoulder blades prickled with every stride he took. Enough guns were fixed on his back to turn him into a human sieve if just one of the renegades was careless. Crossing the open space seemed to take forever. Tar didn't help matters by moving at a turtle's pace despite being repeatedly prodded.

Across the creek, Flavius Harris was as jittery as a hound with fleas. He couldn't wait for his friend to reach safety. To that end, he plunged into the water and waded halfway across so he had a clearer shot at the freebooters.

Davy checked behind him often. Quint and a majority of the cutthroats were edging forward in a ragged line, but so far they were behaving themselves.

"See, Crockett?" Tar said. "My boys are loyal. And greedy. Under my leadership they've taken more bounty in six months than they had in six years. They won't let anything happen to me."

At the water's edge the giant stopped. Davy poked him hard. "Go right across and keep on walking until I say different."

"Getting a jump on my men won't save you. They'll stick to you like glue." Tar hopped off the bank and twisted. "Tell you what. I'm feeling generous. Let me go, and I give my word no harm will come to you or your friends. You'll be free to go, unhindered."

"Worried, are you?" Davy said.

"Not in the least. You're the one who champions lost causes."

"Hush."

Flavius sidestepped so the giant would not come within reach of Matilda. He wouldn't put it past Tar to make a grab for the rifle or try another desperate means of turning the tables. "Hurry," he urged. "Our luck won't hold all day."

Some of the raiders were pressing much too close to Farley and the women. Davy pivoted, sighted on Quint, and warned them to stay back. Reluctantly, they complied, but Quint was fit to be tied.

Taylor gave Heather and Priscilla a pull onto shore. The

matriarch collapsed against him, fatigue and stress combining to weaken her formidable constitution. "Sorry," she blurted. "I'm not as spry as I used to be."

"You're doing fine," Taylor said with pride.

The *caballeros* in the middle parted to permit them to pass. Their gun muzzles never dipped, a fact not lost on the foremost ranks of freebooters.

Per Davy's directions, the horses were tied less than ten yards into the trees. Extra mounts had been brought for Heather and Priscilla, but there wasn't one for the Englishman. Heather solved the shortage by offering to ride double with Priscilla. Davy tied Tar's wrists, and with Farley's help succeeded in boosting the titan up. Once the women were in the saddle, Farley yelled, *"Pronto, amigos!"*

Maintaining their skirmish line, the *caballeros* backed out of the reeds, never once turning their backs to the wolf pack hungry for their hides.

As soon as the hands were under cover, they sprinted to the horses. Farley took control. A yip and a wave of his arm sent the rescuers galloping to the southwest, the Mexicans riding in a column of twos.

In their wake rose heated bedlam as the freebooters rushed to their own animals. Davy motioned at Flavius. "We have to slow them down," he said, reining to the left toward a tall willow. The lowest branches were within easy reach. Snaring one, Davy clambered from the bay and swiftly climbed. Ten feet was enough to give him a crow's-eye view of the meadow. Quint was snarling commands right and left. Blankets and saddles were being thrown onto prancing mounts, cinches tightened, bridles secured.

Planting his feet on a pair of closely spaced branches, Davy braced his back against the bole and raised Liz. The range was approximately one hundred yards. For most, a formidable shot. For Davy, who had won turkey shoots and target contests at distances of one hundred and fifty yards or better, judging the elevation and angle was second nature. He waited until almost all the freebooters were raring to go and a dozen or so had begun to head for the creek.

Quint lifted an arm to signal. His fingers were splayed wide and he was half-turned in the saddle when Liz boomed.

Flavius, watching closely, saw the sea dog's middle finger spurt into the air at the end of a miniature scarlet geyser. Beyond Quint a cutthroat took the brunt of the ball in his rib cage and was flung like a disjointed rag doll to the sod.

Automatically, rifles and pistols were flourished. But a strident cry from Quint prevented a volley from being unleashed. Tar's lieutenant was doubled over in agony, his pumping hand pressed to his shirt, yet he had the presence of mind to keep the free company in check.

Davy cupped a hand to his mouth. "That's your last warning! Follow us and your leader dies!" Without delay he swung from limb to limb to the lowest, slid off onto his horse, and flew like the wind after the Texicans.

Flavius didn't trust the freebooters as far as he could chuck a bull. Again and again he scoured the vegetation to their rear for evidence they were being pursued. Soon he had a crick in his neck that no amount of rubbing would relieve.

Davy was glad his plan had worked. The previous night, shortly after Farley was taken captive, he had ridden back to find Taylor. The Texican had been dead set against his being the one to put his life in harm's way, relenting only when Davy pointed out he didn't know a Spanish participle from a Latin adjective. Taylor could communicate with the *caballeros* where Davy and Flavius could not.

Taking Tar had been Davy's brainstorm, a spur-of-the-moment decision. Insurance, as Tar had phrased it, enabling them to escape with their lives. But Davy wasn't fooling himself about their prospects.

Tar had been right about one thing. The freebooters would stop at nothing to get him back in one piece.

That was Davy's edge. So long as the cutthroats believed he wouldn't hesitate to shoot the giant dead, they'd hold off. What they couldn't possibly know was that Davy had pledged to never again take a life in cold blood. He'd done it once, to spare Heather Dugan and Becky unending misery and abuse. That once had been enough. Guilt would gnaw at his soul for the rest of his days.

Flavius hankered to catch up with the others. He imagined freebooters hard on their heels, imagined them in every shadow, in every thicket, every cluster of trees.

Having the brown stallion under him was reassuring to a degree. Flavius had never owned an animal so splendid. On the grueling ride from the ranch the stallion had never flagged, never displayed the least little fatigue. It possessed extraordinary stamina and speed. Flavius couldn't wait to return to Tennessee and show it off to his wife and kin.

Matilda. Flavius had not thought about her in a couple of days, which was unusual. As much as they had spat and hissed when he was home, he missed her terribly. When they were together they fought like cats and dogs, but when they were apart he pined to be at her side.

Life was strange, Flavius had decided. Try as he might, he could never figure out why the Almighty had seen fit to set the world up the way it was. Having folks suffer like they did, what purpose did that serve? Having them go from the cradle to the grave as ignorant of the true nature of things as they were the moment they popped naked into the cruel world was downright unfair.

Flavius could go on and on. People liked to tease him, joke he was as thick between the ears as he was through the middle, but they misjudged him. Many a time he had lain on a grassy knoll on a sterling summer's day, watching fluffy clouds waft

113

by while wondering about the meaning of it all.

He used to think he had all the answers. All anyone had to do was live by the golden rule and go to church as regular as clockwork to enjoy prosperity and peace their whole life long.

It had come as a shock to learn suffering and death made no distinction between the god-fearing and the godless.

Look at the Tanners. Nicer people you'd never want to meet, yet in recent months Marcy had been kidnapped by Comanches, Walter had died pining for her, and now the family was locked in a war of wits and endurance with a raving band of vicious freebooters. What had they done to deserve any of that? Nothing. Absolutely nothing.

It was a hell of a note, Flavius mused. Being born wasn't an invitation to lifelong happiness. Being born was an invitation to fill a grave.

"It just ain't fair," Flavius said.

"What isn't?" Davy asked. He was surveying the hills ahead for a trace of the Texicans.

Embarrassed by his lapse, Flavius replied, "I was thinking out loud, is all."

"About what?"

Flavius wasn't inclined to say. His pard would only brand him as silly. "Nothing much. Forget it." It was added proof, if any were needed, that pondering the mysteries of life was more trouble than it was worth.

Davy glimpsed the tail end of the column and pointed. "There! Let's catch up." A flick of his reins and a jab of his heels were sufficient to goad the bay into a gallop. Tugging his coonskin cap low, he wound among the trunks with superb skill.

The two *caballeros* at the rear spotted the Tennesseans and let out a yell. Farley Tanner and Taylor, at the head of the rescue party, slowed to a walk long enough for the southerners to join them. From then on, hour after hour, they fled through the pristine wilderness, never stopping, not even to give their tired mounts a breather.

It was Davy's intention, previously agreed on by Taylor, to push on right through the night. By morning they would be within a few miles of the ranch, and safety.

Fate dictated differently.

An hour before sunset, Heather called out in alarm. Davy shifted, anticipating freebooters, but Priscilla Tanner was to blame. She must have dozed off and had half slid from the saddle. Heather's yell woke her up, and she clutched wildly at Heather's back to stay on. Cutting on the reins, Davy brought the bay in alongside their mount and looped an arm around her waist as she started to fall. Her fingers clawed into his shoulders as he swung her clear, then wheeled the bay so he could set her down.

Farley was there in the blink of an eye. "Mother? What's wrong?"

"She's tired," Davy said. And who could blame her? For the past couple of nights she had barely slept a wink. "She needs rest. I say we call a halt until sundown so she can nap."

"Nonsense," Priscilla huffed. "I can hold my own. Give me a minute to catch my breath and we'll be on our way."

Farley startled her by sweeping her into his arms and carrying her to a shaded spot under a tree, where he lowered her as gently as a feather. "You're sleeping, and that's all there is to it." He stifled a protest by pressing a finger to her open mouth. "For once in your life, you'll do as you're told." Smiling, he kissed her forehead. "Please."

"Only because you insist, my dear."

Flavius had to hand it to the Texican. If he were to try bossing his ma around, she'd slap him silly or beat him over the head with a rolling pin. Harris women were noted for their prickly dispositions, Matilda having one of the prickliest.

Caballeros formed a circle around the women and the

horses. Saddles were loosened. Water skins were swapped freely. Jerky was handed out. Little was said, and other than the warbling of a songbird and the sigh of the breeze, the forest was quiet.

Davy and Flavius picked convenient boulders to roost on, Davy taking advantage of the break to reload Liz. "I have some news that might brighten your day, pard," he commented.

Flavius could use some. Ever since their gallivant commenced, one misfortune after another had befallen them. Sometimes he secretly feared they were under a curse, like the one an ancient witchy woman up in the hills had placed on a kinsman. The man's crops had been wiped out by a freak spring flood, his cabin had burned in a bizarre accident, and his one and only plow horse had been consumed by a cougar. No one could convince the kinsman, or Flavius, it was simple coincidence. "What's your news?"

"As soon as this business is finished, we're leaving for home. It shouldn't be more than four or five days, at the most."

If a fly had alighted on Flavius, he'd have keeled over. For ages he'd been trying to extract a firm promise from the Irishman. Always, Davy gave vague or evasive answers, hinting they would head out at such and such a time. Now, at long, long last, he had a definite date. "You won't change your mind?"

"Not this time, no."

"You're not going to back out at the last minute with an excuse to take us to Mexico or Brazil or God knows where?"

"I give you my word. Our wandering days are about over. I've seen enough of the country to last me a lifetime."

"Those freebooters didn't bash you on the noggin when you were their prisoner, did they?"

Davy sighed. He supposed he had that coming, after having

116

dragged poor Flavius over hill and dale for weeks and weeks on end. "No. I'm fine." Plucking a blade of grass, he stuck the stem between his teeth. "I don't need to search anymore."

Flavius cocked his head. "We were *hunting* for something this whole time? Why in hell didn't you tell me, so I could help you look? We might have found it that much sooner."

Smacking the soil, Davy declared, "This is what I was after."

"Dirt?"

"Texas, my friend. Texas. The place where I'll eventually settle down. Where I'll likely end my days."

To say Flavius was confused would be an understatement. "Let me get this straight. We traveled hundreds—no, thousands—of miles. We fought grizzlies, painters, and wolves. We traded lead and arrows with the Fox tribe, the Sioux, and the Atsinas. We almost lost our skins more times than a cat has lives. *And all because you were searching for somewhere to while away your last days in a rocking chair?*"

"That's about the gist of it, I reckon."

Flavius sputtered, then said, "I'd shoot you, but I might need my ammunition later on." He swept their surroundings in disbelief. "What's so blamed special about Texas, anyhow?"

"Where do I begin?" Davy said. How could he explain his fondness for the land, for the people, for the *feel* of it all. "Its size, for one thing. Tennessee is fast filling up. Another ten years and there won't be room for a body to spit without hitting his neighbor."

"You're exaggerating."

"Am I? How many times have you moved in the past five years just so there'd be enough game for your supper pot? Twice, as I recollect." Davy admired a red hawk gliding high in the rich blue sky. "Texas is a hunter's paradise. The people here are friendly. The pace of life is slow. It's everything I've ever wanted. One day, I can't say exactly when yet, I'm coming back here to stay.''

"Those are the good points. What about the bad?''

"For instance?''

Flavius ticked them off on his fingers. "The Spanish, who don't cotton to Americans one bit. The high taxes. Being forced to change religions. And let's not forget the freebooters. So what if we have Tar? The rest will make life miserable for every honest citizen for a long time to come.''

As if to confirm the Tennessean's point, shots shattered the tranquil scene and out of the undergrowth exploded a score of screeching cutthroats. In a fluid crescent they converged on the Texicans. At their head rode Quint, bawling, "Kill 'em! Kill 'em all!''

Chapter Nine

Davy Crockett had figured the freebooters would make a rash attempt to free the Englishman—but later rather than sooner. He'd guessed that Quint and company would ambush them close to the ranch early the next morning. He had erred, though, in failing to take into account the sea dog's impatient nature. Quint and a bunch of freebooters with swift horses had evidently cut out as soon as he and Flavius did, paralleling the Texicans and awaiting their chance. Now they saw it.

As the cutthroats hurtled forward, firing and whooping like a band of Comanches, two *caballeros* fell, mortally stricken. But the rest instantly sought cover, snapping off shots of their own, unhorsing several riders.

Farley sprang to the defense of his mother and Heather, his fancy pistols flashing out. A husky killer bore down on them, sighting along a long rifle, only to take a lead ball in the eye. Another came at them from the right, his shot smacking into

119

a tree behind Farley. The tall Texican's reply was more accurate.

Taylor had dropped to a knee to steady his aim and was shooting just as fast as he could squeeze the trigger and reload.

Acrid gun smoke swirled everywhere. Davy Crockett and Flavius Harris were on their feet in the blink of an eye, Flavius running to his skittish brown stallion to stop it from running off.

Davy spun toward the man responsible for the whole mess. Blackjack Tar had been strangely quiet ever since leaving the meadow. Not once had he given them any trouble. But Davy wasn't fooled. Trying to keep a tight rein on Tar was like trying to keep a leash on a tiger. So long as the tiger sat quietly with its claws sheathed, all was well. The thing about tigers, though, was that at any moment they might transform into raging engines of destruction.

Now the Irishman saw Blackjack Tar dash up behind an unsuspecting Mexican. Tar's hands were bound, but that did not prevent him from clamping them around the *caballero*'s throat. It happened unbelievably fast.

Even as Davy flung himself toward them, Tar's huge arms bulged and he gave a sharp wrench. The *crack* of the Mexican's neck breaking was as loud as a pistol shot. Davy was almost on top of them by then, and he threw Liz high. ''Try me, Tar!''

The giant renegade pivoted. Davy brought Liz sweeping down. The heavy stock caught Tar on the temple in a blow powerful enough to fell an ox. But Blackjack Tar did not fall. Swaying, he staggered, then rallied and lunged, grabbing Liz before Davy could step back. Davy tried to tug loose, but his sinews were no match for those of the giant.

''My turn, raccoon-head,'' the Englishman taunted, and tried to rip Liz from the Tennessean's hands.

Davy cocked the hammer. Liz's muzzle was pointed right

at the giant, low down on his right side. Tar was grinning wickedly in anticipation of taking revenge, but the grin vanished in a haze of smoke when Liz boomed.

From a range of four inches the rifle discharged into the giant. Even a man as massive as he was could not shrug off the impact. The ball ripped through the fleshy outer part of his abdomen below his ribs and ruptured out his back. Tar was jolted backward, lost his balance, and toppled.

Davy whipped out a flintlock. Cocking it, he ran to the stunned giant's side. As Blackjack Tar grunted and pressed a hand to the gushing wound, Davy pressed the flintlock to Tar's ear. "Give me an excuse. Any excuse."

The giant transformed into a marble sculpture, except for a curious quirk of his mouth. "You've got me, mate. Fair and square."

Around them the battle swirled. Seven *caballeros* were down, one convulsing wildly. In a testament to their skill, fully half the freebooters were scattered in attitudes of violent death among the trees. The others had dismounted and were shooting from cover. Quint, unfortunately, still lived, and was crouched behind a willow wide enough to conceal a buffalo.

Davy shifted and prodded Tar to sit up, using him as a living shield. "Quint!" he hollered. "Take a gander over here!"

The sea dog heard. Scowling in livid hatred, the lieutenant took one look, then flapped his arms and screeched over and over, "Stop firin'! All of you! Stop, I say!" One by one the freebooters obeyed. As their shots tapered, so did those of the Texicans. When a cutthroat who didn't hear the order snapped off a last one, Quint's face grew half purple. "Tilson! Damn your bones! Squeeze trigger one more time and I'll have your tongue cut out!"

An unnerving silence gripped the woods. Thick bluish-white

smoke formed small drifting clouds. A wounded man commenced whining like a hurt puppy.

Quint straightened but wisely didn't show himself fully. "All right, you bastard. Now what?" His beady eyes fell to the Englishman's bleeding side. "Cap'n! How bad is it? Are you done for?"

Blackjack Tar swallowed. "I'll live, Mr. Quint. No thanks to your bungling. I thought I taught you better than this. You should have gone on ahead and gunned these fools down from ambush. Not charged them."

"Sorry, Cap'n. Now what do we do?"

Davy moved his arm so the sea dog could clearly see that the flintlock's hammer was back. "I'll decide that. You and your men will skedaddle. Leave your horses and go. Right this minute."

"On foot? Like hell."

"Then Tar dies," Davy declared, jamming the barrel into the giant's skin for emphasis.

Quint was a study in suppressed rage. He cursed lustily, long and loud, then snarled, "You win, you stinkin' landlubber. Me and me boys are on our way. And Cap'n—don't you worry none, you hear?"

"I am counting on you, Mr. Quint," Tar said.

Out of the corner of his eye Davy saw Farley Tanner lean to the left and whisper to Taylor, who in turn whispered to a nearby *caballero*, who then whispered to another, and so on, passing a message from man to man. He gave it no more thought, for just then the freebooters began to back away. Many showed themselves as they retreated around trunks or thick brush.

"You haven't seen the last of us, you scurvy knaves!" Quint promised.

Farley Tanner rose. "Care to bet?" Suddenly jerking a pistol up, he cried, "Now, *companeros*! Now!"

Davy was as shocked as the freebooters. A volley slammed into them, slaying all but four. They sought to flee, but two fell within a few yards, leaving Quint and one other, who scampered for their lives, bounding like fearful deer. Quint plunged into dense growth and disappeared; the other freebooter took a ball in the spine and went down screaming and thrashing until enough lead sliced through him to still his wails.

Blackjack Tar surged erect, heedless of Davy's flintlock, and crouched, ready to hurl himself at Farley. "You son of a bitch!" he roared. "I'll crush you with my bare hands!"

The tall Texican faced the giant and extended a pistol. "Try. Please try, Tar. I want nothing more than to stomp your lifeless face into a pulp. The only reason I haven't killed you already is because hanging you will serve as an object lesson to the trash you ride with."

The giant was incensed almost beyond endurance. He took a half-step, but regained his self-possession in the nick of time. "I won't forget this, Tanner. What you did was outright murder. The same thing you accuse me of."

Davy stepped away from the giant. "As much as I hate to admit it, I agree with Tar. They were leaving. There was no need to slaughter them."

Taylor stepped closer. "I like you, Tennessee. You're an honorable man, and there's a shortage of honor these days. But to paraphase the Bible, there is a time for being honorable and a time for giving those who have no honor a taste of their own medicine." The older Texican sighed. "This isn't a duel we're fighting, Crockett. It's root hog or die. Them or us. And you know damn well they'll stop at nothing to rub us out."

The irony of having one of his own favorite expressions used in argument against him was not lost on Davy. *Root hog or die.* How many times had he said the same thing in similar circumstances? But even during the Creek War, in the thickest of the fighting, he had always fought according to the personal code he wore like a suit of armor: *Be sure you are right, then go ahead.* If his father and his grandfather had told him that once, they had said it to him a million times. And of all their many teachings, it was the one he had taken most to heart.

"I know they will," Davy acknowledged, "but two wrongs don't make a right. You shouldn't have done it."

Priscilla Tanner came from behind a tree. Where other women might have been quaking with fright at their narrow escape, she was ramrod straight and as stern as the day was long. "Nonsense, Mr. Crockett. When you've lived as long as I have, you'll learn there are only two rules in life. One, blood is thicker than water. Two, always get in the first lick—and make it the last."

One of the wounded *caballeros* groaned, ending the dispute. Farley ran to the man as Taylor and others went from body to body, seeing who was alive and who wasn't. Heather stood by herself, arms clasped to her bosom, her features showing she was troubled by something.

Three of the fallen Mexicans still breathed. One shortly died, after asking that rites be said for him by Father Kino. The others were put on their horses. One had to be tied to the saddle, since he was too weak to ride under his own power. Just as a bloodred sun touched the distant horizon, the Texicans resumed their flight.

A somber air gripped the column. Lady Luck had favored them so far, but as Flavius had pointed out back at the creek, they couldn't expect their good fortune to hold forever. Time, and the odds, were on the side of the freebooters.

By design Davy wound up riding beside Blackjack Tar. Someone had to keep close watch over the Englishman, and Davy couldn't fully trust the Texicans. Sure, Farley wanted to see the giant hang to make an example of him, but one of the others might decide, "Why bother?"

124

The giant was uncharacteristically grim, not uttering a peep until stars sprinkled the firmament. The yip of a coyote stirred him from his funk, and looking up, he commented out of the blue, "Pretty night, isn't it, Yank?"

"Never took you for the kind to notice," Davy said without rancor.

"If I am pricked, do I not bleed?" Tar said, and snickered. "I love life, raccoon-head. I love everything about it. When I wake in the morning, the first thing I do is sit up and take a deep breath just to appreciate being able to."

"For a man who likes living so much, you leave a lot of dead people wherever you go."

"Touché," the cutthroat conceded. "But it's not as if I bear them any ill will. Happenstance is to blame for what I am. I didn't choose this path."

"Oh, please." Davy was of the firm opinion that people created their own paths by the conscious decisions they made. If they didn't like who they had become, all they had to do was change.

"Don't believe me, eh?" Tar said. "Well, it's true. I never planned on being a freebooter, Yank. It just worked out that way." He paused. "All I ever wanted from life was to serve my term in the Royal Navy and retire to Liverpool with a small pension to keep me in rum the rest of my days."

"I heard they were going to court-martial you."

Tar's shadowed face grew darker. "The maggots. Believe what you will, I was a damn fine officer, Crockett. I served with distinction. Earned my promotions by the sweat of my brow."

The Englishman stopped, but Davy had the impression Tar wanted to say more. "What really happened?"

A minute elapsed, and Davy was about convinced he had been wrong when the giant cleared his throat. "I made the mistake of angering a high-and-mighty admiral. Not on purpose, you understand.'' His tone grew wistful. ''A nephew of his did me in. I was captain of a man-of-war at the time. The *Royal Prince,* she was called, and a finer ship never was commissioned anywhere. She was a sweetheart.''

''You talk about the boat as if it were your lover,'' Davy joked.

''Spoken like a true landlubber,'' Tar said. ''Lord, you have no idea. I did love her. Hell, I loved being in the Navy. The work was hard and my superiors were demanding, but I thrived. I was so proud of wearing the uniform, once I nearly throttled a fellow captain who had the gall to suggest the Royal Navy was a haven for outcasts and misfits.''

''What did the nephew do to get you into trouble?''

Tar growled like an angered grizzly. ''Hell, it's what the lout *didn't* do. He was a lieutenant fresh out of the academy, a young snot who thought he walked on water and pissed gold. Had connections, you see. The admiral was one of many.''

Davy had met people like that. Politicians, mostly. Arrogant snots who acted as if life owed them a living. Or the taxpayers did.

''From the day we met I never liked him. The blighter waltzed onto my ship and treated her as if she were his. Well, when I set him straight and made him toe the line, he complained to his uncle. I was working him too hard. I was out to get him. The usual rot.''

''The admiral believed his tales?''

''What was that the old hag said earlier? Ah, yes. Blood is thicker than water. What do you think?''

Davy offered no response.

''The admiral wrote to me and asked, ever so politely, if I couldn't maybe go easy on his pride and joy. The nephew had been sucking on the teat of luxury and privilege since he was born, you see, and the admiral would take it as a personal favor if I would go on treating the brat as if he were God's gift to humanity.''

"But you didn't?''

The giant bristled at the memory. "Hell, no. I never showed favorites. Every officer, every man, was treated equally and fairly. I called the bloke into my cabin and gave him what for. Told him if he ever went to his uncle behind my back again, I'd have him swabbing decks from Sunday till hell froze over.''

Davy foresaw the outcome. "He did so, anyway.''

"Of course. But I wasn't worried. So long as I stayed within regulations, I felt I was safe from reprisal.'' Tar's voice dropped to a gravelly rasp. "I was wrong. They waited for an incident they could exploit, then trumped up charges against me.''

"What incident?''

"One of the men was caught drunk on watch. A serious offense. Punishable at the captain's discretion. Since we were in pirate waters at the time, and might have been boarded and overwhelmed because of the sot's carelessness, I had him flogged. Sixty lashes.''

"He lived?''

"Of course. What do you take me for? He was as solid as a brick wall. But I can guarantee he thought twice about taking a nip when on duty from then on.'' The giant tilted his face into the brisk breeze. "Regulations, though, said the most any man could receive was thirty strokes. So the lieutenant reported it to his uncle, and the admiral saw fit to convene a board of inquiry. The whole circus was rigged. I knew I wouldn't get a fair hearing. Just as I knew the admiral would have me thrown into gaol. Or, worse, sent to a penal colony.''

"So you skipped out on your own,'' Davy surmised.

"What choice did I have, Yank? Yes, I busted the heads of my guards and stowed away on a merchant vessel.'' Tar's teeth shone white in the night. "But before it set sail, I paid that squirt of a lieutenant a visit. Broke every bone in his body, I reckon, and left him whimpering on the floor, his jaw shattered in five or six places."

"They'll kill you if they catch you."

"Tell me something I don't know. Why do you think I became a pirate? Deserters are always welcome. Men of my ability are rare and can easily become masters of their own vessels. If not for my falling-out with that bloody Frenchman, Laffite, I'd be on the open ocean right this moment, the deck rolling under me like a sultry wench, the salt air in my lungs, doing what I do best."

Davy had a lot to ponder. There was more to the giant than met the eye, much more. But it didn't excuse Tar for the atrocities he had committed. It didn't atone for the slaughtered innocents. "What happened with Laffite?"

"Bloody hell. Jean claimed I cheated the company out of plunder. But the truth is, Laffite's woman had grown too fond of me to suit him. He wanted me off Galveston Island, so he spread a pack of lies. Now here I am, passing the time of the day with a duffer who wears a coon butt for a hat. God knows, life is strange, Crockett."

The next several miles were covered without comment. As they came to the crest of a rise, Tar twisted. "I was serious before when I said I liked you, Yank. You'd make a fine drinking companion. So I truly am sorry I'll probably have to kill you before too long. No hard feelings, eh?"

"As my grandma used to say, never count your chickens before they're hatched."

The Englishman laughed good-naturedly. "You Americans. I jolly well swear, coming up with stupid sayings must be a national pastime."

For a few warm seconds the two of them shared a special bond that Davy Crockett would never have granted was pos-

sible. A few seconds of friendship, of feeling a common kin-
ship. The interlude was all too short. For barely had Davy
grinned when a darkling shape materialized beside his bay.

"What's going on here, Crockett? Pards with this butcher
now?" Farley Tanner had a hand on the butt of a pistol. "I
thought maybe my ears were deceiving me."

"No one is all bad," Davy said lamely.

Blackjack Tar's smile was gone. "To this young scamp, *I*
am. I'm all the evil in the world. I'm Attila the Hun and the
bloody Khan rolled into one. I'm the worst human being who
ever lived in the whole history of the world. Isn't that so,
Texican?"

"You said it, not me," Farley answered.

"So be it, then," the giant said, and without warning he
lunged, sending Davy flying from the saddle and into Farley,
whose draw was a fraction too slow. The flintlock cleared
Farley's belt but went off prematurely, the shot missing Davy
by a whisker and whizzing into thin air.

Laughing lustily, the Englishman reined into the forest. Instantly, Mexicans streamed after him. Davy, flat on his back
with the bay prancing nervously on one side and Farley's
mount trying to stomp him on the other, could do nothing.
Yells rippled along the column as Farley applied his spurs and
raced on around the bay.

Davy heaved up from the grass, grabbed the saddle horn,
and hauled himself astride his mount. He started to go in pursuit, then abruptly hauled on the reins and simply sat there,
listening to the crash of brush and the giant's coarse mirth
recede rapidly to the west. He didn't look to his right when
another horseman arrived.

"What happened? Why are you just sitting there?" Flavius
asked. The commotion had brought him on the fly, in dread
his friend had been harmed.

More Mexicans clattered into the night.

Flavius was confused by the Irishman's lack of interest. "It's Tar they're after, isn't it? Shouldn't we help? We're better hunters than they are any day of the week."

"We don't have to bother," Davy said.

"Why not, pray tell? What do you know that I don't?"

"If Tar gets away, he'll be back."

"What makes you so sure?"

"We licked him. We made him eat crow in front of his whole band. Now he has to kill us, whether he wants to or not. He has to show his men he still has what it takes to be the top dog."

The explanation only added to Flavius's confusion. "Wait a minute. What do you mean, 'whether he wants to or not'? He's slain women and children, for God's sake. Why would he think twice about making wolf meat of us? We're nothing to him. Enemies, to be snuffed out at his leisure."

"Are we, you reckon?"

Flavius dogged his friend's steps as Davy trotted on down the line to where the women tensely waited. Over half the men, including Farley and Taylor, were gone. *Now would be an ideal time for the freebooters to strike*, Flavius mused, resting Matilda across his thighs. He realized Priscilla was speaking and tried to pay attention.

"—believe that polecat gave us the slip. If there's any justice in this world of ours, my son will catch him and finish him off once and for all. It's what my Walter would do. What I would do."

Heather Dugan, who had hardly said two words since her rescue, now piped in with. "Yes, you Texicans are strong believers in justice, I've noticed."

Priscilla turned. "Do I detect a hint of reproach?"

"More than a hint. I can't get over how your son ordered those freebooters to be shot down in cold blood. And now you want him to kill an unarmed man?"

"Hmmmm." The matriarch was thoughtful. "I credited you with more sand. A Tanner doesn't get all squeamish over squashing a few bugs."

"Men aren't insects."

"These aren't butterflies we're talking about, dear. These are two-legged cockroaches. And I don't know about you, but when I see a cockroach in my house, I smash it." Priscilla laid a wrinkled hand on the younger woman's shoulder. "This isn't St. Louis. The social amenities don't apply here, Heather. There's little law to speak of, and the courts of final appeal are hundreds of miles away in Mexico City. So when we have to, we hold our own court and save the government the expense."

"See? Even you do it."

"Do what, child?"

"Justify the endless killing by claiming it's your only choice. If you ask me, you're simply making excuses to justify behavior no civilized person would ever condone."

Priscilla was a long time replying. "Tell me. When those freebooters were pawing you at their camp, when they were drooling over you and doing things not fit for a lady to repeat, did you want them dead?"

"That was different."

"I don't think so. If you'd had a gun, you'd have shot every last one. You didn't care about them being taking into custody or being held for formal trial. You wanted those shiftless vermin to pay. What my son did today, and what, God willing, he might do now, is no different from what you wanted in that meadow. Judge not, Heather, lest you be judged."

Crackling undergrowth heralded the return of Farley and Taylor and the men who had gone with them. "We lost him, damn it," Farley declared, then brought his horse in close to the Irishman's bay. "And I hold you partly to blame, friend.

I saw how you were treating that filthy beast. For all I know, you let Tar escape.''

''I did no such thing,'' Davy said.

Farley was inclined to debate the point, but Taylor interceded. ''It's no use fighting among ourselves. Pretty soon we'll be up to our necks in freebooters, when all the rest show up, and we'll have all the fighting we can handle.''

''How long, do you reckon?'' Priscilla asked.

''Depends on whether they're leery of jumping us at night and wait until broad daylight.'' Taylor scanned the heavens. ''Our only hope is to ride like the wind and pray we reach the ranch before they catch us.''

''Then why are we sitting here squabbling?'' Priscilla demanded. With a smack of her hand, she and Heather were off, leading the way, sparking a headlong rush into the vastness of the Texas night.

Davy Crockett found himself shunned by the Texicans, *Americanos,* and Mexicans alike. They treated him as if he didn't exist. Which, by noon the next day, might well be the case.

Chapter Ten

By midnight it was apparent they would never reach the Tanner *rancho* by morning. The horses were winded, severely in need of rest. Priscilla was worse off. She gamely clung on to Heather and tried to stay awake, but her chin constantly drooped and she couldn't keep her eyes open for more than a minute.

Davy Crockett didn't say anything. Not at first. He felt Farley should be the one to call a halt. The son stayed close to his mother at all times and was aware of her condition, as the many worried looks he cast at her proved. Yet Farley never acted. Davy waited, and waited, and around one in the morning decided enough was enough. Urging his horse up next to the tall Texican's, he got straight to the point.

"What in tarnation has gotten into you? Do you want Priscilla to fall off and crack her noggin?"

Farley was still upset about the incident with Tar. "You have no say in this anymore. None at all."

"Fine. Be that way. I'll bring fresh flowers to lay on your mother's grave."

Glowering, Farley sped on. But not for long.

The thickest of the woodland was behind them. Scattered hills dotted a broad plain split by arroyos. For some time Taylor had been rising in the stirrups now and again and intently scouring the murky terrain as if in search of a landmark. Suddenly he hollered and reined to the right, bringing them to the rim of a shallow basin half an acre in extent and carpeted by high grass.

"What do you think?" the older man asked after they stopped. "It's the best we're liable to find. Large enough for all of us and the animals, yet small enough that we can hold our own for as long as our ammunition lasts."

"We'll only stay here until first light," Farley said. "Then we light a shuck. The *hacienda* can't be more than twenty-five miles away."

The news sent a ripple of apprehension down Flavius's spine. He'd calculated it couldn't be more than ten. "Might as well be the moon," he absently said, and was treated to glares from Farley and Taylor. Their motive eluded him until he saw anxiety afflict Heather.

Davy kneed the bay into the basin, slid off, and roved the rim. A small arroyo slashed the plain forty yards to the east. To the south the nearest cover was a stand of cottonwoods. To the west it was a hill two hundred feet distant. To the north the woodland ended just beyond rifle range. Taylor had picked wisely.

Farley posted the *caballeros* at regular intervals. Each had a loaded rifle and a brace of pistols. As Davy watched them spread out and lie prone, it dawned on him he didn't know a single one. The Tanners had never introduced him.

Here they were, risking life and limb together, brothers in peril, as it were, and they were complete strangers.

Smiling, Davy cradled Liz and went to the closest, holding out his hand. The Mexican was puzzled but shook it warmly. Davy said his name and learned the *caballero* was called Juan. In turn he shook hands with each, repeating their names so he would be sure to remember them. Stocky Carlos. Dapper Dominguez. Dark, deadly Baca. Pleasant Chaves. Friendly Mariano. He met them, one and all, and flattered himself they sincerely appreciated the gesture.

As he walked from *caballero* to *caballero* he noticed little things about them and their style of dress, things he had overlooked. Most, for instance, wore bands of tinsel cord on their *sombreros*. Their jackets, or *chaquetas,* sported fancy buttons and braids. The outer parts of their pants flared open from the hip to the ankle and had been decorated with buttons or lace. Many wore bright sashes around their waists. Some favored *serapes,* blankets with holes in the middle, thrown over the shoulders and worn with their heads poking through the holes.

They presented dashing figures, these *caballeros.* Carefree, strong, independent, filled with zest for life.

No less dashing were their horses. As befitted men who spent most of their lives in the saddle, they spared no expense in the equipment they used. Big, heavy saddles lavishly embossed with silver were the norm. So were solid silver bridles, spurs with rowels five inches long, and gaily decorated saddlebags.

If this was the day he would die, Davy mused, he could not do it in finer company. He took his position at the southeast corner.

"What was that all about?" Flavius asked. The Irishman was forever doing peculiar things. It was part of what made being his friend so interesting.

"I figure if we're due to show up at the Pearly Gates together," Davy said, "we might as well line up in alphabetical order."

"If you don't beat all," Flavius said, and meant it. The notions his fellow Tennessean came up with boggled his brain. There were times when Flavius half suspected Davy had twice the brainpower of most men—or was partly addlepated.

The waning hours of night passed uneventfully. Slowly the inky black lightened to a deep blue, which brightened as the eastern sky was suffused by radiant bands of orange and yellow. The wolves ceased howling, the coyotes stopped yipping. Robins and sparrows and larks greeted the new day merrily.

Through it all, Priscilla slept the sleep of the dead. She was so exhausted, she would not rouse when Farley tried to awaken her shortly before dawn. "Mother? It's time for us to go."

"Let her be," Heather said. "Another five minutes won't hurt."

The Texican faced the woman he had been on the verge of proposing to when his life came crumbling down around him. "Something is bothering you. I can tell."

"We'll talk about it later."

"Later?" Farley said wryly. "Awful optimistic."

"Just know this, Farley Tanner," Heather declared. "Whatever happens to us, I have never loved anyone more than I love you."

Davy saw the Texican open his mouth to reply, but a shout from Taylor brought the peaceful interlude to a crashing end.

"Here they come, *muchachos*! Get ready!"

A dust cloud to he northeast signaled that the moment of truth had arrived. Soon the cloud hovered over a high hill on which stick figures were silhouetted. As the freebooters swarmed down the slope they resembled a horde of ants. They grew in size quickly, into solid ranks, ten wide and eight or nine deep, nearly ninety of the worst killers to ever tread soil.

The *caballeros* rose onto their knees, their rifles resting on the basin's rim. Farley stood at the northeast corner where the brunt of the charge would be, a pistol in each hand. "Don't fire until I say so," he hollered, and smirked. "Not until we can see the whites of their eyes."

There was no mistaking the rider at the forefront. Blackjack Tar's bulk was akin to that of a hulking Cyclops out of antiquity. His cloak flew in his wake like the mane of a fierce African lion.

In and of himself the Englishman was the most formidable man Davy Crockett had ever met. Davy glimpsed the giant frequently as the renegades threaded through the woods. When they burst out of the trees, Tar elevated an arm, bringing them to a halt.

Taylor had his cheek tucked to the stock of his rifle. "If only he'd come closer," he said. "Just a little closer, is all I ask!"

The giant shrugged the cloak off his right shoulder. "I'll say this for you. You've tried your best." His resonant voice carried to the basin without Tar having to yell. "Out of respect for the ladies, I'll make this as easy on you as I can. Surrender, and I'll have each of you shot, military fashion, by a firing squad. Swift and merciful. What do you say?"

Farley laughed bitterly. "I say . . . go to hell!"

"Think of the women, Tanner," Tar replied. "You have my solemn vow they'll be shot dead. No one will manhandle them."

"You're all heart."

"Mock me if you must. But I don't make offers like this lightly, and I never make them twice. It's now or never. Give up and die a manly death. Or resist to the last, and I swear by the Queen's throne that any of you who survive will wish you hadn't. Then my men will get to amuse themselves with the females. Your mother is old, but I'll warrant she still has some vim and vinegar left in those old legs of hers."

Farley Tanner pointed a pistol. Fire-red, granite-faced, he wanted to shoot so much, his entire body shook from the violent emotions buffeting him. His lips curled in a savage grimace, he challenged his nemesis. "Quit trying to talk us to death. Show us what you're made of, Tar. And we'll show you how Texicans die."

"Fool!" the giant said. "So be it."

Eternity was measured in heartbeats. The *caballeros* had the grave air of men who knew beyond a certainty of a doubt they were going to die and were prepared to sell their lives as dearly as possible. Davy scanned the basin and remarked offhandedly, "I wish we could fight in the open. I don't much like being hemmed in."

A roar from Blackjack Tar was the catalyst. Whooping lustily and brandishing their guns, the freebooters rolled toward the Texicans, a great roiling tide, a thunderous host hell-bent on total destruction of their enemies.

"Aim at the first row," Farley barked. "The first row only!"

On came the freebooters, shrieking their fury, a living tide washing over the plain. Lathered horses and grimy riders blended into one, into fierce centaurs gone amok, unstoppable, invincible in their numbers. Or were they?

"Now, boys! Give 'em hell!"

A dozen rifles spoke in a united din. Sixty yards out a dozen cutthroats pitched from their mounts or were slammed backward and clutched for slim support. The charge slowed, those in the second and third ranks thrown into confusion. But only briefly. The freebooters came on again, their compact formation ragged though still intact.

"Reload!" Farley commanded.

Flavius Harris was attempting to do just that. But he had never been so scared. Those screaming visages, reeking of blood lust, were terrifying to behold. *This is nothing like the Creek War,* he thought. Back then the fighting had been done in thick swamp or verdant forest. Half the time he hadn't seen the Creeks at all and just fired when everyone else did.

Here Flavius could see his foes clearly. He could see their blazing hatred, their contorted features. They were a great snarling, motley throng of hardened killers, intent on ripping him to shreds. Or worse. It filled him with fear so potent, his hands shook as if he had a case of the winter shivers. Concentrating for all he was worth, he poured in black powder and rammed a ball and patch down the barrel.

By then the freebooters were so close, Flavius swore he could see the whites of their eyes. When Farley Tanner rang out the command, he aimed on a scraggly screeching target and fired in unison with the *caballeros*.

Davy Crockett, however, did not. The second volley cut into the cutthroats like a scythe into ripe grain. Another eleven or twelve were brought to a lurching and in most cases final halt. Their horses, riderless, either stopped cold or veered, sowing more confusion and causing the middle ranks to rein up short.

Among them was Blackjack Tar. As freebooters on the left and right swept wide to come at the basin from the east and the west, the Irishman focused on the Englishman to the exclusion of all else.

Davy held his breath. Lining up the front sight with the rear, he fixed both squarely on Blackjack Tar's broad chest. His trigger finger tightened slowly, smoothly, just as it should. Liz cracked and kicked.

At that exact split second another freebooter astride a plunging mount blundered in front of the giant. The ball intended for Tar's heart smashed into the other man instead. Smashed into him and through him, for Davy saw Blackjack Tar's expression of surprise as the ball, its momentum largely spent, slammed into Tar's right shoulder with enough force to twist Tar half around and partially unseat him.

If there had been any lingering doubt in Davy's mind that the freebooters would protect their leader at all costs, it was dispelled when those surrounding the giant closed around him, shielding him and assisting him in righting himself even as they guided him to the rear.

The center of the attack had been broken, but the wings were now closing in, twenty horsemen to a side. Farley, still standing straight in defiance of the leaden hail, ordered the *caballeros* on the right side of the basin to fire at the cutthroats to the east, while those on the west side were to handle the other wing.

One of the freebooters, Davy saw, held a large curved sword on high. A scimitar, he seemed to recollect. Plainly this was another pirate, one who should never have forsaken the ocean blue for the rolling prairie, for the man was nowhere near enough to use his exotic sword when Davy's next shot splattered his head half over creation.

Other rifles blistered the air with fire and smoke. The cutthroats to the east were decimated and had the wisdom to break off before more were lost. Those on the west, however, weathered an accurate firestorm poured into them by the *caballeros* and hurtled on toward the rim, determined to do or die.

Flavius happened to glance over a shoulder as a scar-faced freebooter on a plunging piebald sailed into the basin, a pistol in each brawny fist. A *caballero* pivoted to shoot him but was felled first. Automatically, Flavius brought up Matilda and let fly. He did not think to aim, but the shot kicked the man off the piebald as if bashed by an invisible hammer. Grasping his powder horn, Flavius began to reload, pausing when his ears registered an awful sound—a disturbing quiet, a quiet so silent it was as if he stood in his own grave deep under the earth.

The freebooters had been repulsed, leaving fully a score of broken bodies to litter the battlefield. For their bravery the Texicans paid dearly. Four more *caballeros* were gone. Four more, when not one could be spared.

So thick was the cloud of smoke drifting sluggishly on the limp wind that Davy could not see the tree line for quite a while. When he could, the next stage in the clash was revealed. The renegades were not inclined to risk another frontal assault. Not anytime soon, at any rate. Fires were being built. Forty or so ruffians were making themselves comfortable close to the woods while the rest fanned out, ringing the basin in an unbroken line. Just out of reach of even the best marksman, they dismounted and hunkered.

"They're fixing to wait us out," Taylor said. "All they have to do is sit out there and let thirst and hunger weaken us. Three days from now they'll ride in and finish off those of us who are still alive."

"Then we won't wait three days," Priscilla Tanner stated. "We'll learn them a thing or two. We'll charge the bastards and bust out of their trap."

In all the excitement Davy had forgotten about the matriarch. Neither she nor Heather had been harmed, thank goodness, although one of the dead *caballeros* had been kneeling an arm's length from Heather when a stray bullet brought him low.

Miraculously, Farley was unhurt. Not once during the fight had he ducked down, yet none of the many shots fired at him scored. A charmed life, some might say. A reckless soul, others would say. Or a brave man who would defend his loved ones with his dying breath.

A water skin was passed around. Davy drank sparingly; the water might need to last days.

Flavius was thirsty enough to gulp every last drop, but he followed his friend's example and reluctantly relayed the skin to a *caballero* without doing more than wetting his lips. "Shut up," he said under his breath to his growling stomach. Food was the least of his worries.

"What's this?" Taylor abruptly said. "What the devil are they up to now?"

Advancing unarmed from the north was Quint, holding aloft in his right hand a tattered white shirt tied to the end of a crooked branch. The sea dog had a rolling gait typical of those who called the sea home. A thumb hooked in his belt, he waved the branch and hallooed. "Will you respect the flag of truce or no? I have words from me master."

Farley climbed to the top. "No harm will come to you. But keep your hands where we can see them."

Growing cocky, Quint sashayed into the leveled muzzles of the *caballeros*. "Surprised you're still among the livin', Tanner. The Cap'n has put a hundred-dollar bounty on your head."

"Tell him it will cost him dearly to collect."

Quint surveyed the basin and responded, "Looks to me as if your gall has already cost you dearly, Yank. So tell you what. Surrender, and the Cap'n promises a merciful death. Same as before. Except he'll let the women go free. On his honor as a former officer in the Royal Navy."

Farley snorted. "A Comanche has more honor in his little finger than Tar has in his whole body." The Texican gazed at the activity to the north. "And I thought Tar only made the offer once. Let me guess. You lost more men than you counted on. That has some of your *amigos* upset. They're complaining. They want to call it off. So Tar throws us this bone to spare himself a mutiny."

"Rubbish," Quint said, but his tone and countenance belied it. "The Cap'n is just feeling generous, is all. Like that time he spared those babies at the Jenkins place." The sea dog's smile was as oily as whale blubber. "So what do you say, mister? Do I tell the Cap'n you'll lay down your arms?"

Farley moved too fast for the eye to register. His right hand closed on Quint's Adam's apple and squeezed like a vise.

142

Quint, in a panic, dropped the white flag and punched at Tanner's chest and face, to no effect.

Davy ran up the slope, almost to the top, in case freebooters rushed to the lieutenant's aid. None did, although oaths and threats rent the morning.

"Here is what you can tell your lord and master," Farley snarled, shaking the sea dog as a panther might a rat. "Texicans never surrender. Ever. You will pay dearly for every drop of blood you spill." Shoving Quint, Farley dumped him on his posterior in the dirt. "Let Tar know that he's sadly mistaken if he thinks it will be easier from here on. It won't be. It will be harder."

Quint was rubbing his throat and gasping for precious breath. "You had no call!" he railed. "I was under a white flag."

"Take the flag and—" Checking himself, Farley clenched his fists. "Crawl back to Tar and repeat everything I told you. And add this. Say that once everyone learns what happened here—and they will—once they hear how a handful of Texicans stood up to a freebooter army and killed more than anyone ever has, the hold you have on Texas will be broken. No one will fear the freebooters ever again."

Quint started to rise, but Farley took a step, jabbing a finger into the sea dog's ribs. "I told you to *crawl* and I meant it." His hand streaked to the smooth butt of a pistol. "Crawl like the maggot you are. Crawl all the way back to your friends."

"All the way—?" Quint croaked.

The Texican pointed, and the freebooter did what anyone who had a hankering to live would do. Rolling onto his stomach, Quint snaked northward, mumbling nonstop. When he had gone twenty yards, he looked back. Farley began to draw the pistol, and pointed again. Quint took the hint.

Flavius shook his head in astonishment. "These Texicans sure can get their dander up," he said softly.

143

"No one can ever accuse them of not having the real grit," Davy agreed. "Put enough Texicans together and they could lick just about anyone. These freebooters, the Spanish army, you name it."

"What makes them so wolfish, you reckon? Shucks, even old ladies like Priscilla are prickly pears."

"Life here does it, I'd guess," Davy said. "Life everywhere shapes how we grow, what we become. We're like hot lead poured into molds. How we turn out depends on what kind of mold we're poured into."

Flavius had to think about that one. Just then a *caballero* called out. Quint had risen and was sprinting for the woods with remarkable alacrity. Farley Tanner's pistol glinted in the bright sunlight, but for a reason Flavius couldn't fathom the Texican didn't shoot.

Cutthroats cheered Quint on. Upon safely reaching them Quint turned and made an unmistakably crude gesture at Farley.

Taylor pumped his legs, gaining the rim. "This one's on me," he said, carefully elevating his long gun.

"It's too far. Don't waste the lead," Farley cautioned.

"Watch." Taylor licked his thumb, then wiped the front sight clean. Squinting, he gazed along the sights and adjusted the angle he held the rifle. He was about set when the sea dog moved toward Blackjack Tar, who sat propped against a tree. "Dog my cats," Taylor muttered, and swiveled.

Quint was broadside to the basin. The range had to be two hundred yards. Even Davy would be hard-pressed to make it. He watched Quint as the lieutenant jabbered at the giant. Hardly had the conversation commenced when the crisp retort of Taylor's rifle punctuated it.

Most of the freebooters looked to see who had fired, Quint among them. His spindly arm lifted to shield his face from the sun and was still lifting when his feet were flung out from under him. A tremendous howl wavered on the wind as renegades rushed over and discovered Taylor's shot had deprived them of their lieutenant.

Farley smiled at the older man. "You shouldn't have done that."

"You're welcome, I'm sure."

"I meant it. Now Tar will never hear the message I sent."

"Oh." Taylor chuckled. "Sorry. I plumb forgot."

A general flurry in the enemy camp resulted in scores of freebooters taking rifles and spreading into a skirmish line. They dropped to the ground and edged closer. Taylor gripped Farley and pulled him into the basin, saying, "Appears we riled them a mite. We'd best dig in to weather the storm."

His forecast was accurate. Presently, the renegades began peppering the basin with steady rifle fire. Three-fourths of the shots hit the rim. Some kicked up geysers on the slopes. But enough penetrated the bowl to make moving around risky.

Everyone, Flavius included, glued themselves to the sides and prayed they were spared. He came close to jumping out of his skin when a ball thudded into the earth near enough to spray his cheek with bits of grass and dirt. "I don't like this at all."

Neither did Davy, but short of going to the freebooters with an engraved request to stop, what could he do? In one respect it worked in their favor, since it was unlikely the freebooters possessed an unlimited supply of ammunition. Every bullet expended was one less that could be used later.

Flavius had long since reached the limit of his forbearance. "I swear in the name of all that's holy. If the good Lord see fits to let us make it home alive, I am never leaving Tennessee again. Get someone else to go gallivanting with you."

Hadn't his friend been listening last night? Davy wondered. This was his last gallivant. Hearth and home would be the rule from here on, until the kids were grown and Elizabeth and he were free to do as they chose. Then maybe his cherished move to Texas would be in order. The freebooters would be long gone and the situation with the Spaniards would be settled. I would be safe enough.

Muffled thuds gave him something else to think about. His right ear was flush to the sod, and the thuds he heard were being conducted through the soil. "What the—?" he exclaimed, comprehension coursing through him like a lightning bolt.

"No!" Davy said, and shoved up high enough to see over the rim. The gunfire he'd assumed was in retaliation for Quin had another purpose. It had kept them pinned down while the freebooters snuck in close enough to rush the basin.

Which they had just done.

Chapter Eleven

"Come on, men!" Davy Crockett hollered. "The freebooters are upon us! Give them hell!" Suiting action to words, Davy hiked Liz and sent a ball through the forehead of an onrushing renegade.

Flavius Harris sprang up and fired without conscious thought. He didn't bother to take aim. Consequently, he was all the more pleased when a charging figure clutched at its chest, buckled at the knees, and was still.

The Texicans responded superbly. Instantly at the rim, they extended their rifles. Taylor was the first to shoot, and as always his marksmanship was unerring. Farley Tanner unleashed both of his expensive pistols, one after the other. With each retort a freebooter was pitched into oblivion.

As for the *caballeros,* they rallied and cut loose on all sides, a withering volley that ripped into the cutthroats like a hurricane into cane, shattering sternums and skulls, and leaving many of their enemies writhing in torment or forever motionless.

The freebooters returned fire, but their shots were rushed and wild. Few struck the defenders. Chaves was one of the luckless ones, tumbling down the slope, never to smile again. And a horse whinnied and staggered, a crimson hole in its foreleg.

A grizzled killer urged his companions on. "At 'em, boys! Don't stop now!" But the brunt of the surprise attack had been blunted. Another flurry of shots was exchanged, then the freebooters hastily gathered up their wounded and frantically backpedaled.

The Texicans wisely did not waste lead. Once the brigands were almost out of range, they stopped shooting. A wounded *caballero* was promptly tended to. So were three hurt horses.

Farley Tanner beamed with pride at the Mexicans who were risking their very lives on his behalf. "I've never been more proud to be your friend, *amigos,* than I am right this moment. If I am killed, I will go to my reward grateful for having friends like you and richer for having known you."

Heather Dugan had been huddled next to Priscilla, screening the older woman with her own body. Now she stepped to Farley and warmly hugged him, saying, "Don't talk like that! Nothing is going to happen to you. I won't allow it."

The desperation in her tone touched each of them, especially Davy Crockett. It reminded him of Elizabeth, of his wife's unending love and devotion. Devotion he had stretched to the limit by being away for so long. She had every right to be furious. But knowing her, she would never bring it up. She had a deeply forgiving nature. She was, quite literally, too good for him.

Farley embraced Heather. "I've got something to say. And I want all these men to hear it." He licked his dry lips and swallowed. "I wanted to do this right, under the starlight, on bended knee. But we were interrupted the last time, so we'll have to make do.'' Farley kissed her passionately, then declared, ''Heather Dugan, I would like to have the honor of accepting your hand in marriage.''

Priscilla had tears in her eyes. Not all the *caballeros* spoke perfect English, so those who did had to translate for those who did not. When they were done, every last Mexican moved below the rim and stood, out of respect for their *companero,* Farley, and for the sanctity of that special moment.

Heather had rested her forehead on the tall Texican's chest. Now she looked up, her face aglow with an inner light, her eyes shimmering, and answered huskily, ''I accept your proposal, my gallant gentleman. I will be your wife. And for as long as we shall live, I will always be at your side.''

They kissed again, fire and love and lust combined, a kiss that lingered, a kiss such as few are ever privileged to witness.

''Tarnation,'' Flavius said. ''I wish Matilda would pucker me like that. She never uses her tongue.''

Davy did not tell his friend that Elizabeth had showered many such romantic kisses on him. Rare guilt afflicted his conscience. Except for hunting trips and the like, he would never leave her alone for long spells again.

A new sound brought the happy interlude to an end. Everyone climbed to the rim for a cautious look-see. The freebooters were in the woods, busy as bees, the steady *thump-thump-thump* of axes biting into wood punctuating the buzz of activity.

''They're chopping down trees,'' Taylor said.

''Why? For firewood?'' Priscilla asked. ''Maybe they have a notion to smoke us out somehow.''

Taylor's mouth pinched together. ''No, I'm afraid Tar is much more savvy than I gave him credit for. My guess is the worst is yet to come. By late this afternoon they'll make one last try to wipe us out. And this time we won't be able to stop them.''

"It's not like you to roll over without half trying," Farley mentioned. He gazed intently into the woods. "What is it you reckon they're up to, anyhow?"

"They're making themselves bulletproof."

"Hell. That's not possible, is it?"

"We'll have to wait and see."

That was the hard part. The waiting. Minute after minute of nervous tension, of emotional strain. Davy tried to relax, to snatch a few winks of sleep, but his traitor body refused to cooperate. His nerves were as raw as an open wound.

The ring of axes never ceased, not once from the time it started until the hot hours of middle afternoon when the forest finally fell ominously still. A lot of yelling took place. Tar's voice, mostly, but he was too far away for the words to be clear.

Taylor took to pacing, a bad sign in itself. Davy had reckoned him as among the most rock steady of men. Farley and Heather were locked in each other's arms, just lying there, cheek to shoulder. Priscilla dozed off and on.

Only the *caballeros* were their usual carefree selves. They had a remarkable knack for taking everything in stride. Idly talking and joking, they acted as if they were in their favorite *cantina* rather than huddled in the middle of the sprawling wilderness waiting for death's dark hand to claim them.

By Davy's estimation it was shortly past three when stocky Carlos gave a yell. Movement along the tree line had drawn his interest. Freebooters were everywhere, constantly bustling about.

Flavius saw something that startled him. "What the devil are those?" he blurted. Almost forgetting himself, he began to straighten above the rim for a better view. "They look like pieces to a fence."

"More like portable walls," Davy amended. "To protect them from our slugs so they can get in close to us."

"Oh."

A chill filled Flavius as the devious scheme became clear. The freebooters had chopped down dozens and dozens of saplings and long limbs and intertwined them into crude but impressive wooden barriers, or shields. Each was eight or nine feet long and six to seven feet high. Gaps afforded handholds for the renegades to hold the shields in front of them.

"Sweet Jesus," Flavius breathed. The barriers were thick enough to absorb most any lead thrown, just as Davy had said. "All they have to do is waltz across that field and we're done for."

"Are we?" Davy said, turning his face into the wind. It was blowing from the southwest, a scorching arid breeze that parched a man's throat and made him wish he were soaking in a cool creek.

"Maybe we should make a run for it," Flavius suggested. "While enough of the horses are healthy."

Davy motioned at the freebooters who still surrounded the basin. "How far do you figure we'd get, pard?"

Not far at all. Flavius gulped and watched as the barriers were lined up in a long row from east to west, each practically brushing the edges of those next to it. *No!* He just couldn't accept that in another ten minutes he would be a lifeless husk. "Sorry, Matilda," he said under his breath.

Davy raced along the bottom of the slope to Taylor. "I have a brainstorm," he announced, and urgently imparted it. "A long shot, I know. But it might work."

"Even if it doesn't, it will slow them down. Let's try."

From the Irishman's possibles bag he extracted a fire steel, his flint, and a small tin of punk. No woodsman worthy of the name ever went anywhere without them. They were as important to survival as a reliable knife. Next to knowing how to rustle up food, the ability to make a fire was the most essential skill a frontiersman mastered.

Taylor bent to tear at clumps of dry grass. "Gather as much as you can!" he advised the *caballeros,* who diligently did so. A sizable pile was made at the top of the north rim.

All this time the freebooters were busy. At a bellow from Blackjack Tar they practiced advancing a few steps at a time while bearing the barriers. They coordinated their efforts so they maintained a straight, even row.

Davy observed everything they did. His timing was crucial. Too soon, and the nasty surprise would peter out before reaching them. Too late, and the renegades would reach the basin before any damage could be done.

Tar appeared at the east end of the wooden shields. His side was bandaged, as was his shoulder, but he showed no evidence of weakness or fatigue. "I warned you!" he thundered. "Now you'll pay, damn your souls! And for killing my mate Quint, I'll make all of you suffer as no one has ever suffered before."

It was no idle boast, Davy reflected. The rogue titan had perfected torture to a fine art, if the gory tales told about Tar's exploits were to be believed. Upending the punk, Davy shoved the tin into his leather bag, then held the flint and fire steel in either hand. Desperate straits called for desperate measures, and theirs was as desperate as could be.

"Nothing to say, Tanner?" the giant taunted. "How about you, coon butt? No final words for posterity?"

Farley heaved to his feet, waving his pistols. "Pay us a visit, bastard. I'll do my talking with these."

"Get down!" Taylor rotated and leaped, tackling Tanner and bearing him to the slope as several rifles cracked. Slugs buzzed overhead, sounding exactly like bees in flight. "Have a care, my young friend," Taylor said. "He did that on purpose so you would show yourself."

"Yet another one I owe him," Farley said through clenched teeth.

Davy never took his gaze off the barriers. Tar, smirking smugly, had stepped behind them again, and at a clipped order the entire line slowly moved forward. The freebooters kept step with one another, military fashion. Neatly executed, it would turn the tide in their favor.

"What are you waiting for, Crockett?" Taylor asked.

"Not yet," Davy said. The wind—the most crucial factor of all—had slowed somewhat. Lowering the flint near the punk, he marked the progress of the moving wall. The freebooters were fifteen yards out from the trees, their shields tightly positioned, Tar calling cadence. Then twenty yards, but Davy didn't move. Thirty yards, and he glanced at the punk.

"Now!" Taylor called.

Davy didn't listen. At thirty-five yards he stroked the steel against the flint, producing sparks that fell on the punk. Others might take ten or twenty strokes to succeed, but the punk ignited on that first stroke. Tiny flames flared, flames he fanned with light breaths. Expanding swiftly, the flames licked at the pile of dry grass and it immediately caught.

Once the wind took over, the fire spread with astounding speed. The pile was engulfed in moments. From there the flames spread rapidly outward, devouring whole tracts of high grass in the blink of an eye.

Weeks before Davy ever tangled with the Comanches and wound up in Texas, he had barely survived a prairie fire caused by lightning. The conflagration had covered a front stretching across hundreds and hundreds of acres, and he would never forget how those flames leaped across the plain with dazzling, deceptive speed. He counted on that now.

The freebooters came briskly on, Tar's booming voice rising above the creak and rattle of their shields. A few shouts arose as smoke appeared, and the fire could be seen consuming wide swaths. But either Tar didn't see the flames, which was improbable, or he had every confidence his men would reach the basin quickly enough to foil Davy's ruse.

The giant miscalculated. The renegades were two-thirds of the way across when waist-high flames erupted directly in front of them and hungrily licked at the saplings and branches. Some of the barriers burst into flame. Others smoldered. Thrown into a panic, fully half the freebooters tossed their shields down and fled.

The rest, though, particularly those at the east end, held firm, buoyed by Blackjack Tar's presence and threats. More than enough to slaughter the defenders, could they but reach the bowl without further mishap.

"Fire at will!" Farley directed.

The *caballeros* had been waiting to do just that. Slugs battered the constructs like hail, but the freebooters never slowed or swerved. A cutthroat dropped here, another there, nowhere near enough to whittle them down to where they had to abandon their assault. Most of the shots were harmlessly deflected.

Davy Crockett gripped Liz. It had been a smart idea, but it had failed. Now it was do or die, and the devil take the hindmost. All the *caballeros* had moved to the north side of the basin, leaving the east, west, and south rims vulnerable. But it couldn't be helped. The freebooters behind the barriers were the greater threat.

In the midst of the bedlam, with the butchers sixty feet out and closing fast now, Farley Tanner turned to Heather Dugan and clasped her hands in his. "I never wanted it to be like this. If the Lord had been willing, I'd have made you the happiest woman alive."

"You already have." Heather locked her lips to his as the freebooters opened fire. She went on kissing him while the ground around them was pockmarked by lead. "My lover. My life."

Farley looked deep into her eyes, then shoved her at his mother, grasped his pistols, and entered the fray. At that distance his .55-caliber smoothbores were powerful enough to punch through the shields, and they did, a pair of screams attending each shot.

Davy fired and set to reloading, his fingers flying. The *caballeros* sent a stream of slugs at the walls and many scored, but nowhere near enough to stem the inevitable. In another minute the freebooters would reach the rim and it would all be over.

Vaguely, Davy was aware of a lone cutthroat off to the west who had turned to flee but halted halfway to the forest. The man was screeching and jabbing a finger to the southeast. Then Davy noticed others doing the same. Puzzled, he risked a glance, and a thrill coursed clear down to his toes.

Forty horsemen were sweeping toward the battlefield in precise order, arrayed in battle formation, their glittering lances held upright. The sun gleamed off sterling buttons and spurs, glinted from an armory of pistols and swords.

"The lancers!" someone cried.

Yes, the lancers. Captain Jose Barragan barked an order and the forty cavalrymen broke into a charge. Another crisp yell, and the Spaniards lowered the weapons for which they were famed, holding the long sturdy shafts wedged to their sides.

A cheer was torn from the *caballeros*. Davy added his voice, but he didn't leap for joy as some did. The timely arrival of the patrol was a godsend but not surefire salvation. Seventy or eighty freebooters were left—far too many.

Captain Barragan was taking an awful chance, a chance only a man of tremendous courage would contemplate. Their charge was truly magnificent—but potentially disastrous.

The cutthroats who were on the south side of the basin were the first to feel the sting of those lethal tips. Engrossed in the conflict, they didn't awaken to the threat at their rear until the lancers plowed into them. Renegades were transfixed in their tracks. Without breaking stride the Spaniards sheared through the line, slanted around the corner of the basin, and bore down on the wooden breastworks.

Davy saw Captain Barragan smile, saw the officer voice a command that resulted in the troopers urging their mounts to greater speed. Freebooters scattered before them like mice before cats. But not those behind the barriers. They stood their ground, poking rifle muzzles and pistols through random openings.

The resultant crash was deafening. Barragan and his lancers smashed into the shields at a full gallop, splintering some, shattering others, their lances piercing through to inflict terrible carnage among the freebooters. But the cutthroats gave as good as they got. Flintlocks spat smoke and slugs. Troopers reeled in the saddle, or fell.

"Help them, boys!" Farley bawled. "Give them cover!"

Eagerly, the *caballeros* resorted to their rifles. But many of the renegades who had fled were rushing back, and a constant discharge of guns was whittling the lancers down one by one. Fifteen of the valiant cavalrymen were down or dying when Captain Barragan, who had dropped his shattered lance and was wielding a sword with ruthless efficiency, shouted a string of Spanish that resulted in the lancers wheeling their chargers and dashing toward the basin. Freebooters rushed to cut them off but were forced to retreat in the face of a brutal pounding by the Texicans' guns.

Davy darted to the right to permit the retreating troopers to gain sanctuary. Barragan bid two of his men keep hold of the horses while the rest lined the slopes, mingling with the *caballeros*.

The *capitán* himself sank to his knees between Davy and Farley Tanner. His uniform was spattered with gore and his boots bore bright scarlet speckles. Winded, he grinned and said in his thickly accented English, "That was something, eh? God willing, I will live to tell my grandchildren."

Farley put a hand on the other man. "I take back everything I've ever said about you, Jose. You risked your life for us. I'll never forget it."

"Please, don't get maudlin," the officer replied. "I was doing my job, nothing more, nothing less. We heard gunfire from far off and came to investigate." Removing his hat, he wiped a sleeve across his slick brow. "Had I known it was you, I would have thought twice about rushing to the rescue."

The tall Texican laughed. "Poke fun all you want. The Tanner family never forgets a friend."

Barragan glanced at Davy. "Do you hear him, senor? A week ago I was the cow droppings he scrapes off his boots. Now I am his friend. Life is strange, is it not?"

Flavius Harris overheard. "You don't know the half of it." The firing had tapered off while both sides licked their wounds and regrouped. The freebooters were engaged in a general withdrawal. Few of the makeshift shields were still intact, and those that were had mostly been abandoned. Twice as many bodies littered the field as before, some twitching, some convulsing, some of the fallen weeping or moaning or begging for help.

Davy surveyed the aftermath and hung his head. The more he saw of warfare, the less he liked. War was the last resort of idiots, his grandma had once said. And she was right. "I wish I may be shot," he remarked, "if I'm ever dumb enough to get caught up in a war again."

Captain Barragan replaced his hat. "A fine thing to say to a professional soldier, senor. Fighting is my stock-in-trade." He examined his bloody sword. "A trade at which I am quite competent. Which is why I say to you now that we must decide how soon to attack these *bastardos*. Based on my experience, I say within a very few minutes. While they are still disorganized.''

Flavius turned. ''Did I just hear rightly. You want *us* to attack *them?*''

''*Sí.*''

''I don't see any such thing,'' Flavius said. ''They still outnumber us by twenty to thirty or better. We'd give a good account of ourselves, sure, but all you'd do is get us wiped out to the last man.''

''You misjudge them, senor,'' Barragan said. ''These are not brave *hombres* we are talking about. Freebooters are killers and thieves and cowards. Men who would rather stab you in the back than in the stomach.''

''So?''

''So it is not necessary to slay every last one. All we need do is crush their spirit and they will turn tail like the yellow dogs they are.'' The officer nodded at the battleground. ''We have hurt them, senor. Hurt them severely. Another such beating and the day will be ours.''

''Says you.'' Flavius thought he was beginning to understand why Davy was so partial to the people here. They came up with as many crazy ideas as the Irishman did.

Taylor had joined them. ''I have no objection. Anything is better than waiting around for them to do us in. There's only one problem.''

''What might that be?'' the officer asked.

''We're mighty low on ammunition. Some of the men are down to their last five balls. Baca only has three left. Mariano has one.''

Barragan snapped a finger and a lancer snapped to attention at his side, ready to do his bidding. ''We have a limited supply, too. But what we have I am willing to share with the *caballeros.*''

Davy had not offered his opinion yet, preferring to weigh

what everyone else said first. Sitting up, he added his two cents' worth. "Why throw more lives away? In three or four hours the sun will go down and we can make a run for it. They'll never catch us in the dark."

Heather did not surprise anyone by agreeing. "He's right. There's no need for anyone else to die." The loving gaze she bestowed on Farley Tanner showed she had a particular individual in mind.

The Spaniard sniffed. "Begging your pardon, senorita. But this is best handled by the men. Do not trouble your pretty head about it."

"My pretty—?" Heather said, and would have lit into him like a riled she-cat had Farley not snagged her wrist. "Why, you pompous goat. It's men like you who give all men a bad name."

Captain Barragan took the abuse in stride. "Please, senorita. I understand that you are under great stress. But this is hardly the proper time or place for feminine theatrics."

To his dying day Davy Crockett firmly believed that if Heather Dugan had had a gun in her hands at that moment, she'd have blown Jose Barragan's head clean off. She definitely looked at Farley's as if considering helping herself to one of his. Fortunately for the Spaniard, one of the *caballeros,* dapper Dominguez, called from the rim, "Senors! Someone comes."

A lone freebooter bearing the same truce flag used by Quint was nervously approaching, taking tiny steps, as scared as a jackrabbit near a den of wolves. He held his other arm out from his side to demonstrate he was unarmed. Licking his lips every few steps, he would glance back at where Blackjack Tar stood holding a rifle.

"What are they up to now?" Taylor wondered.

"Must be a trick, maybe to distract us," Flavius feared.

Davy doubted it. All the freebooters were assembled at the

159

tree line, waiting for the messenger to convey his message. Was it his imagination? Davy asked himself, or were many of the renegades scowling openly at their leader? What did that portend?

Farley moved higher so the messenger could see him. "That's far enough, mister. Say what you have to say from there."

Relief etched the man's swarthy face. "Thank you! Please tell your men not to shoot! I don't have a weapon, not even a knife."

"Get on with it," Farley demanded. "What do you want?"

"Mr. Tar wants to end this once and for all. His exact words."

"And how does he propose we do that? By surrendering? Hasn't he learned yet we never will?"

"No, sir. He doesn't want you to give up. He'd like to settle this in personal combat. Man to man, he said. For honor's sake. Just him and one other. No guns allowed. What do I tell him?"

"Hold on," Farley replied. "I want to be sure I follow you. Tar expects one of us to walk out there and fight him to the death?"

"Yes, sir."

Flavius and some of the *caballeros* laughed long and loud, and were hushed by a gesture from Farley. "Does Tar have someone special in mind?" His tone hinted that he hoped it would be he.

"He sure does, sir. The feller he'd like to fight to the death is the one he calls 'coon butt.' I believe his real name is Davy Crockett."

Chapter Twelve

There are moments in our lives we never forget. Experiences so intense, so special, they are forever branded in our memories. It might be something as simple as a favorite dish served by our mother or an aunt when we are young, rice pudding so delicious it is the standard by which we measure all rice pudding the rest of our lives. It might be the first time we ride a horse. Our first kiss. Our first date. Or it might be a tragedy. The death of a loved one. A broken bone we suffer. Even something so ordinary as the first time we are stung by a bee.

Davy Crockett had many such special memories. And for as long as he lived he would never forget this moment, either. The instant when all eyes in the basin swung toward him. When everyone there, including himself, mirrored surprise at Blackjack Tar's choice.

His first thought was *Why me?* Of all of them, he was the only one who had struck up a halfway friendly conversation with the giant. The only one who had treated Tar halfway human. But he was also the one who had shot Tar. Not once. Twice.

Flavius Harris was stunned almost beyond words. He didn't rightly understand why the Englishman had picked his friend. He did know, though, that under no circumstances would he let Davy walk on out there. Not when they were days away from heading for home. Not when he felt certain he couldn't make it back alone. To the messenger he shouted, "Forget it! Tell that overgrown slug he'll get no such satisfaction from my pard! What do you take him for, an idiot?"

"Tar won't be happy," the freebooter said.

Farley answered. "We don't care how he feels. There's no need for Crockett to accept the challenge. Not when we now have enough men and ammunition to make you sorry you ever tangled with us."

"Believe me, mister, we're already sorry. We've lost more good boys than we ever counted on. More than we could afford to. Now, most of us just want to get the hell out of here. But Tar insists on having this fight."

"Tell him to forget it. And tell your friends that a lot more of them are going to die before this day is done."

The messenger looked back at the giant. "Damn, mister. I hate being the bearer of bad tidings. He's liable to stomp me into the dirt."

"There's an old saying in these parts. You make your bed, you have to sleep in it. Savvy?"

"All right. I'll tell him." Dejected, the freebooter turned to go.

The matter had been settled. Tar's request had been refused. Davy Crockett had been spared from having to fight a virtual Goliath. All he had to do was stand there and watch the messenger slink back to the trees and the incident was over. That was all he had to do. Yet, the next instant, he opened his mouth and called out, "Hold on, hoss. This is Crockett. Go and let your master know I accept."

"What? You do?"

Once more Davy was the focus of attention. Several people tried to talk at once. "What in the hell are you trying to prove?" Taylor demanded. Farley said, "You're loco. He'd smash you like a bug." Heather Dugan shook her lovely head, saying, "Don't do it, Davy. The risk is too great."

As for Flavius Harris, he could feel the blood drain from his face at the mental image of his best friend being torn limb from limb. "Why in the world did you do that? Think of Elizabeth and the kids."

Davy was thinking of them, and of all the mothers and children in Texas who were just like them. Innocent home-steaders who stood to lose their lives if Tar was allowed to go on ravaging the countryside. Dozens more to add to the giant's tally. "Tar is the brains of that outfit. Without him, they won't cause half as much grief."

Captain Barragan scratched his shin. "You have a point, senor. Until the Englishman came along the freebooters were not well organized. Their raids were few and far between. Kill him, and you chop off the head of the serpent, eh?"

Taylor objected. "I can't believe I'm hearing this. Tar is twice as big as you, Davy. Probably three times as strong. He'll break you like a dry twig."

"He's a man. Nothing more. Nothing less."

Farley placed his hands on his hips. "This is a hell of a note. If anyone has a right to fight Tar, it's me. It was my ranch he attacked, my mother and my fiancée he stole. He killed men who work for me, men who were my good friends. Let me go in your stead, Crockett."

"He wants me," Davy said, and moved toward the rim.

Flavius was not about to permit it. Barring the Irishman's

path, he declared, "I can't let you. I'm sorry, but if you take another step, I'll box you on the ear."

"Please, pard."

"No. Never."

They stared at each other. The best of boon companions, they had known each other since childhood. As kids they had played tag and other games. They had idled away many an hour at favorite fishing holes. They had hunted birds and rabbits with slingshots. Later, Davy had been best man at Flavius's wedding. Flavius was considered an uncle by Davy's children. Each had an abiding affection for the other, affection nurtured by their many years together. There was nothing one would not do for the other one.

Which made it all the harder for Davy to turn to Captain Barragan. "I'd be obliged for a favor."

"Say no more, senor. I understand." The officer snapped commands. Before Flavius quite suspected what was happening, four lancers were on him, seizing his arms and tearing Matilda from his grasp.

"No!" Flavius resisted, pushing one of the cavalrymen away and rotating on the balls of his feet to slug another. He cocked his arm, then hesitated when a hand fell on his arm and the man he loved like a brother spoke softly.

"Don't. Please. For my sake."

The lancers recovered, holding Flavius fast. Frustration and baffled fury rocked him as he watched Davy hand Liz and both flintlocks to Farley Tanner. "If you get yourself killed, I'll never forgive you."

Davy grinned wryly and winked. "I'll never forgive myself. Give my love to my family, in that case. Tell Elizabeth—" He paused. "No. No need for that. Most of the time she knows what I'm thinking without me having to say a word. Just say my last thoughts were of her and let it go at that."

Flavius had to cough to clear a lump from his throat. "Will do."

Nodding at the Texicans, Davy made to leave but stopped when Captain Barragan said, *"Uno momento, por favor."* The officer held a shiny small dirk, doubled-edged and deadly. "I keep this hidden up my sleeve. To use as a last resort. Perhaps it will come in handy."

Davy accepted the five-inch weapon, hefted it, then removed his coonskin cap and placed the dirk inside. He was careful not to spill it out as he replaced the cap. Pulling on the coonskin, he verified that the dirk rested snugly on his hair. "I'm obliged, Jose. I'm sure Tar will have a few tricks up his sleeve."

"Do you want my sword as well?"

"No." Davy patted his tomahawk and his butcher knife. "I'm used to these. They've saved my bacon more times than I care to recollect."

"But they are so short, and the Englishman will have his cutlass. You need a weapon with greater reach."

Davy did not know what to do. Barragan was right, but he had never even held a sword, much less relied on one in the heat of battle. Gingerly, he accepted the hilt and executed a few short jabs and thrusts. It was lighter than he had anticipated, easy to handle, but he was still unsure of what to do.

"Take it," Flavius said.

"You think?"

"Weren't you the one who once told me that in a scrape every weapon helps?" Flavius had relaxed, and the lancers no longer held him as tightly. But they would not let him go until instructed to do so. Which was a shame. He'd like nothing better than to give his friend a parting hug. And he had never hugged a man in his life. Not even his own pa.

Davy Crockett smiled, then quickly spun and scaled the slope. The messenger was back among the freebooters, talking to Blackjack Tar. Davy advanced, but warily, suspiciously. He wouldn't put it past Tar to lure him out into the open so a marksman could pick him off.

The giant waved at him, as if they were the best of chums, then gave a pair of pistols to another renegade. Striding several yards out onto the charred grass, Tar faced his men and bellowed for all to hear, "This is between the Yank and me. No one is to interfere. If I win, I'll drag his carcass back and let you hack it to bits. If he wins—leave, mates. Head for the Gulf. Enough of us have gone to Davy Jones's locker this day."

Davy scoured the prairie. The fire he had started had petered out in most spots shortly after it reached the line of shields. A finger of flame to the west had penetrated to the woods but lost momentum on a wide patch of bare ground. It was just as well. He would hate to think he had been responsible for burning thousands of acres and destroying countless wild creatures.

Blackjack Tar had squared his shoulders and was coming to meet him. More than ever, Davy was awed by the former officer's sheer size. The breadth of those shoulders, the rippling muscles on Tar's corded arms and wrists, his imposing height, all were enough to instill fear in any foe. Tar walked with a swagger, as supremely confident as a grizzly in his unrivaled strength. His massive physique radiated power and vitality as the sun radiated light and heat.

In addition to the cutlass held in his right fist, Tar had a long knife in a leather sheath on his left hip. Wedged under his belt near the big brass buckle was a club of some kind. Short and thick, it had a solid knob at one end, and a thick handle. Davy had never seen the like, and he assumed it must be from Tar's days in the Royal Navy.

The giant wore a faintly mocking smile. He had removed the bandage on his shoulder but not the one on his side, which was caked with dried blood. No hint of pain or discomfort marred his craggy countenance. He was as fit as could be, a monster of a man in the prime of life.

Halting ten feet away, the Englishman glanced at the basin. "So which one of those scurvy Texicans is going to shoot me when the time is ripe? That young jackass Tanner, or clever old Taylor?"

"Neither. It's between you and me. As you wanted."

Tar rested the blunt side of the cutlass on his shoulder. "I'll be honest, coon butt. I never reckoned you'd agree. Never took you to be so stupid." Much too casually, he took a pace to the left. "Why'd you take me up on it? False bravado? Curiosity?"

"I would like to know why you picked me, yes," Davy admitted.

"It's simple, Yank." Again the colossus slid to the left, his deceptive smile contradicting the cold glitter in his piercing eyes. "You and your bunch have about ruined me. My men are ready to find themselves a new leader. They blame me for this." Tar gestured at the many bodies slowly bloating in the terrible heat. "The cost is too high, they think. So they wanted to call it quits."

"Why didn't you take their advice?"

Blackjack Tar sighed, then frowned. "I wish to hell I could, Crockett. But if I tucked my tail between my legs and ran off to lick my wounds, I'd be showing weakness. And in the free company, to show weakness is the worst thing you can do. The weak are preyed on by the strong. It's dog eat dog. Someone would be bound to challenge me."

"So? You'd win."

The Englishman chuckled. "Thanks for the confidence, Yank. Yes, I would. No one has ever beaten me. Not once. But there are plenty now who question my judgment. Who think I'm not fit to lead. Even if I fought off all challengers,

I stand to lose half of those who have licked my boots for so long. I intend to keep them under my wing.''

Davy was holding the sword low down, against his right leg. When Tar shifted again, so did he. ''Is that where I fit in?''

''Sharp, coon butt. Very sharp of you. Yes, that is where you come in.'' Tar chewed on his mustache. ''It's like this. I needed to show my men I still have what it takes. Challenging one of you to a duel to the death was the best way. They'll see me cut you to pieces, and it will give them second thoughts about deserting.''

''But why *me*?'' Davy pressed. ''Why not one of the others?''

''Ah.'' Tar slid slowly to the left while pretending to be interested in a pair of crows winging overhead. ''Well, Taylor is too damned clever to suit me. I wouldn't put it past him to hide a gun up his shirt and shoot me. Farley Tanner is a hothead. Reckless. Rash. That makes him unpredictable and doubly dangerous.''

Tar grinned. ''You, on the other hand, are as easy to read as a book. You're an honorable man. Someone who would never shoot an enemy in the back. Never fight dirty. The kind of man I can count on to play by the rules even when there are no rules. That's your weakness. That's what will do you in.''

''You seem to have it all figured out.''

''The only reason I have stayed alive as long as I have is because I am always two steps ahead of those who would feed me to the fishes. Most rate me as a big brainless stump, but I'm as clever as Taylor. Hell, I'm smarter than the whole lot of you combined.''

Davy shifted again. ''And more modest.''

Laughing lightly, the giant tapped the cutlass against his upper arm. ''There's one final reason I asked for you.'' He pressed his other hand to the bloody bandage. "You shot me, you son of a bitch. I was careless and paid the price. Now I have to even accounts or my men will think anyone can hurt me and get away with it."

There was another lesson Tar should have learned from being shot but hadn't, Davy mused. "Is there anyone you'd like us to notify afterward?"

"After what, Yank?"

"After I kill you. Any next of kin? Any friends?"

With blinding speed Blackjack Tar sprang, slashing the cutlass at Davy's face. In sheer reflex Davy brought up Barragan's sword to block it, but so powerful was the blow, so incredibly strong was the giant, that Davy was knocked backward and nearly fell.

Tar was on him in a flash, raining cut after cut. Davy parried and countered awkwardly, unaccustomed as he was to the finer points of sword fighting.

The Englishman hissed like a viper. Redoubling his frenzy, he sought to break through Davy's guard. Davy backpedaled, pure instinct keeping him alive as he automatically deflected slash after slash.

Steel rang loud on steel. From the freebooters rose a loud sustained cheer. Tar was a whirlwind, his cutlass whistling to the right and the left. "It's only a matter of time, Yank," he gloated.

Davy was inclined to agree. Already his arm was tired, his shoulder sore. He could not hold out forever, not against the giant's formidable brute force. In order to prevail he must rely on his wits, not his sinews. So, as Tar elevated the cutlass for yet another swing, Davy suddenly ducked and hacked sideways at the giant's shins. He was off balance or he would have inflicted more damage. The sword's keen edge bit in deep, but not deep enough to cripple.

As it was, Blackjack Tar howled like a banshee and leaped

out of reach. Blood flowed freely over his pants and boots "Dam you!" he roared. "I'm going to slice off your ears and nail them to the mainmast!"

Davy barely braced himself before the giant unleashed another onslaught. The cutlass was everywhere, arcing down on either side or straight at his head. Again and again and again Davy warded it off, a whisker's width all that separated him from eternity.

The Englishman's failure to end the fight swiftly seemed to anger him. He became reckless. His swings were wider, more open, leaving his midriff exposed. In a frenzy he sought to batter the Irishman down, rearing over the Tennessean like a mighty bull gone amok.

Then it happened. A resounding blow jarred Davy just as he flung himself to one side. Losing his balance, he stubbed his foot in a clump of grass and fell onto his right side. The sword went flying.

"At last!" Tar exclaimed, pausing and raising his cutlass in both immense hands. "I'll split you like a melon."

Davy clawed backward, but the giant came after him. He knew that if he touched his tomahawk or his knife, the cutlass would descend.

"Take off that stupid hat, Yank," Tar commanded. "I want to see your head burst."

The coonskin hat! Davy removed it and clutched it to his chest, as if in mortal dread, his right hand sliding inside to grasp the hilt of the Spanish dirk. "You've won!" he cried and cringed, acting horrified.

"That I have!"

"Then again—!" Davy said, lancing the dirk out from under his cap—straight into Blackjack Tar's groin.

In total shock, the giant gawked down at himself. He was frozen in place, not moving even when Davy wrenched the dirk out and scrambled to the left to gain room to rise. Tar gurgled, his visage growing the hue of a bright beet. A low rumble started deep in his barrel chest and rose bit by bit in volume, finally erupting from his throat as a titanic roar. Eyes wide and wild, he launched himself at the Irishman in a berserk fit.

Davy hurled the dirk at Tar's neck, but the giant swatted it with the cutlass. The next stroke nearly took Davy's head off. Pivoting, Davy flourished his tomahawk and his butcher knife. When the cutlass arced toward his temple, he parried with the butcher while simultaneously angling the tomahawk at his adversary's forearm. He connected.

Being wounded a second time had a sobering effect on Tar. Recoiling, he crouched and rasped, "So you do fight dirty, after all. I should have known. Your being American, and all." A scarlet stain spread along his sleeve. "For every drop of blood, you'll suffer a thousand agonies."

Idle threats were a waste of energy. Davy had learned that lesson from earlier scrapes. So rather than respond, he circled, holding the tomahawk and the butcher down low so Tar couldn't predict where he would strike next.

The freebooters had fallen silent. To a man they were riveted to the tableau, their futures hanging on the outcome. On the rim of the basin many of the Texicans had appeared, side by side with Barragan's lancers. Neither faction brandished weapons. Both were willing to let the personal combat decide the outcome.

Blackjack Tar pounced, delivering a swipe that would have cleaved Davy in half had it landed. Skipping to the right, Davy saved himself, then retaliated by thrusting his knife into the renegade's shoulder.

Tar jumped a full yard to the right. "You're like a damn cat! I've never met anyone so fast." For the first time since they met, doubt crept into his eyes. Doubt, and something else, something new to Tar. He tried to poke fun by jesting, "I guess I should have picked that fat friend of yours.'' But he wasn't fooling anyone, least of all the Tennessean.

"You should have left when your men wanted you to.''

"What would you say if I did it now? If we call it quits? I'll just turn and walk off. You do the same. Me mates and I will ride off without another ounce of blood being shed. We'll let bygones be bygones.''

"No.''

"Why not, Yank?''

"It's gone too far.''

"Please, coon butt. As a personal favor. I have no real desire to kill you.''

Davy avoided a rut as he resumed circling. To stand still was to invite another attack. "That's where we differ,'' he said. "I want nothing more than to put an end to your reign of terror. And if the only way to do that is to put an end to you, so be it.''

Tar was quiet a minute, brooding. "I've seldom been so wrong about anyone as I have about you. Very well. As every old salt knows, you can only walk the plank once. So let's end this. No holds barred.'' His hands moved a little higher on the hilt of the cutlass. "Let's go out like men.''

Davy halted. His weight was evenly distributed on both feet, his legs were bent at the knees. He had the knife at his waist, the tomahawk slanted crosswise in front of his chest. He was ready. As ready as he would ever be. "Do it.''

The Englishman did a strange thing. Abruptly straightening, he touched the cutlass to his brow in a formal salute. Then he crouched again, snarling like the beast some claimed he was. The cutlass flashed on high. In a blur it drove downward.

Davy was not there when the long blade split the space he had occupied. A bound took him in close. A flick of his left arm buried the butcher knife in Tar's thigh. Staying in motion, spinning, he whipped the tomahawk in a backhand that caught

Tar completely off guard. The blade sheared into the giant's left wrist, through skin and flesh and deep into the bone.

Tar grunted. That was all. Retreating a few yards, he grimaced and pressed his ruptured limb to his chest. Copious amounts of red gushed over his shirt. "Damn!" Tearing at his cloak, he ripped it off and frantically wrapped it around his arm.

A horse nickered to the north. Some of the freebooters were departing. Others hung their heads.

"Well, isn't this a fine kettle of fish?" Tar said gruffly. Swearing, he flung the cutlass down. "Ever wondered how I earned the nickname 'Blackjack,' Yank?" With his right hand he brandished the short club. "Once I was the best in the Royal Navy."

Davy was prepared for a rush. Or so he thought. But the giant was on him in half a heartbeat. That club, or blackjack, or whatever it was, wove an intricate pattern that no man could defend against. Davy brought up the butcher knife, only to have his knuckles brutally pounded. His hand instantly went numb and the butcher fell.

That left Davy the tomahawk. He countered with a series of skillful feints and punishing smashes, but it was soon apparent Tar had made no idle boast. With a blackjack the Englishman was unbeatable. Severely wounded, slowly bleeding to death, still the giant was more than holding his own; he was winning.

Davy swung the tomahawk at the Englishman's jugular. Midway, his hand was met by the blackjack. It felt as if he had just been stomped on by a buffalo. He started to lose his grip but grit his teeth and held tight. Tar hammered him on the shoulder, on the ribs, above the ear. Bells rang inside his skull.

The blackjack slammed into his temple. Blackness engulfed the world, and Davy tottered. He blinked, saw the giant about to deliver what might be the last blow of all. His head throbbing, he threw himself backward while pumping his right arm. The tomahawk flew from his fingers.

Scores of hours had been spent practicing that toss. Davy could hit the center of a man-size target from fifteen paces nine times out of ten. In this instance the tomahawk spun end over end and thunked into the center of Blackjack Tar's forehead.

Jumbled confusion ensued. Fleeting vertigo brought Davy to his knees. Shots cracked from the vicinity of the basin. Footsteps rushed in his direction. Strong hands slid under his shoulders and hauled him upright.

"You did it, pard! You did it!"

A slap to his cheek cleared the fog from Davy's mind. He saw the freebooters fleeing, saw mounted lancers and *caballeros* in pursuit. Someone clapped him on the back. He looked down into the empty eyes of the giant.

"Tar's dead!" Flavius hollered. "The rest are running. It's over! At long, long last it's over and we can go home."

"Home," Davy Crockett said, and never in his life had a simple word sounded so sweet to the ear.

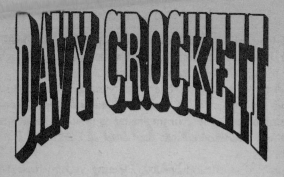

DAVY CROCKETT

Sioux Slaughter. With only his long rifle and his friend, Davy Crockett sets out, determined to see the legendary splendor of the Great Plains. But it may be one gallivant too many. He barely survives a mammoth buffalo stampede before he's ambushed—by a band of Sioux warriors with blood in their eyes.

___4157-X $3.99 US/$4.99 CAN

Homecoming. The Great Lakes territories are full of Indians both peaceful and bloodthirsty. And when the brave Davy Crockett and his friend save a Chippewa maiden from warriors of a rival tribe, their travels become a deadly struggle to save their scalps.

___4112-X $3.99 US/$4.99 CAN

Dorchester Publishing Co., Inc.
P.O. Box 6640
Wayne, PA 19087-8640

Please add $1.75 for shipping and handling for the first book and $.50 for each book thereafter. NY, NYC, and PA residents, please add appropriate sales tax. No cash, stamps, or C.O.D.s. All orders shipped within 6 weeks via postal service book rate. Canadian orders require $2.00 extra postage and must be paid in U.S. dollars through a U.S. banking facility.

Name_____
Address_____
City_____State_____Zip_____
I have enclosed $ _____ in payment for the checked book(s).
Payment <u>must</u> accompany all orders. ❑ Please send a free catalog.